CAVALL
IN CAMELOT

QUEST
FOR THE
GRAIL

GAWALL
IN CAMELOT

QUEST FOR THE GRAIL

AUDREY MACKAMAN

HARPER

An Imprint of HarperCollins*Publishers*

Cavall in Camelot #2: Quest for the Grail
Text copyright © 2019 by Audrey Mackaman
Illustrations by Cory Godbey
HarperCollins Children's Books, a division of HarperCollins Publishers,
195 Broadway, New York, NY 10007.
www.harpercollinschildrens.com

Library of Congress Cataloging-in-Publication Data

Names: Mackaman, Audrey, author. | Godbey, Cory, illustrator.
Title: Quest for the Grail / Audrey Mackaman ; illustrations by Cory Godbey.
Description: First edition. | New York, NY : HarperCollins, 2019. | Series:
  Cavall in Camelot ; #2 | Summary: Cavall the deerhound must lead King
  Arthur and his friends deep into the forest on a quest for a legendary grail
  with magical healing properties.
Identifiers: LCCN 2019000126 | ISBN 9780062494535 (hardback)
Subjects: | CYAC: Quests (Expeditions)—Fiction. | Dogs—Fiction. |
  Wolves—Fiction. | Arthur, King—Fiction. | BISAC: JUVENILE
  FICTION / Animals / Dogs. | JUVENILE FICTION / Legends, Myths,
  Fables / Arthurian. | JUVENILE FICTION / Action & Adventure /
  General.
Classification: LCC PZ7.1.M24547 Qu 2019 | DDC [Fic]—dc23 LC record
  available at https://lccn.loc.gov/2019000126

Typography by Joe Merkel
19 20 21 22 23   PC/LSCH   10 9 8 7 6 5 4 3 2 1

First Edition

To families, whatever form they take

IGHT HAD COME TO CAMELOT, BUT CAVALL couldn't sleep. It felt like every strand of fur on his body was on end, waiting for something, like the moment right between the lightning bolt and thunder.

The royal bedchamber was dark and peaceful. Beside him on the rug, Luwella lay absolutely silent and hardly moving. Even in sleep she maintained her wolfhound's poise. On the bed, Gwen and Arthur were likewise sound asleep, their breathing steady yet mistimed with each other. No restless tossing. No crying out. Their dreams were peaceful.

Why was he the only one who seemed on edge?

Maybe if he rolled over . . . No, that didn't help. But maybe if he tried another position . . . No, that didn't work either.

"Be still," Luwella groaned, not bothering to open her eyes. "It is difficult enough to sleep in this heat without you fidgetink." She then muttered something about how summer was not so hot in her homeland before rolling over.

Cavall sighed. Perhaps Luwella was right and he couldn't sleep because it was too warm in the room. He scooted off the rug and flopped onto the cooler stones. That seemed to work for a while, until the waiting-for-thunder energy built up and shot into his long, gangly legs. Maybe he just needed to work that energy out.

He kicked out in one direction. Then rolled over and kicked out in the other. Then rolled onto his back and began kicking with all four legs at once while twisting from side to side.

"What is that beast of yours doing?" Gwen cried.

"Go to sleep, Cavall!" Arthur said with a groan.

Chastised, Cavall rolled back onto his stomach and laid his head between his front paws. He vowed that even if he couldn't fall asleep, he would lie here, perfectly still, until morning. He could manage that. He could be a good dog.

As he lay there, staring at his paws, he felt a flea moving on his back haunch. And, well, he couldn't just leave it. He turned and gnawed at the itch. The flea tried to hop away, and Cavall chased after it, down his leg to his back paw, until he caught the critter. Then he had to scratch the itch it had left behind and lick his fur back into place and . . .

"I never knew a dog could *lick* so loudly," Gwen complained.

The bedsheets rustled, and Arthur sat up. "I'll see to it." His bare feet hit the floor, and he stood with a groan.

Cavall sat up as his person padded over to him, bringing the familiar and comforting scent of wild rivers and gentle rain. He always felt so special when his person's attention was on him, whether it was a scratch behind the ears or a kind word. Cavall couldn't stop his tail wagging furiously.

Arthur let out a yawn and leaned down. "You're keeping us awake, you know." The thumping of Cavall's tail ceased as Arthur grasped him by the collar and led him out of the room. With a "sorry, boy" and a pat on his rump, the king of Camelot closed the door and returned to bed.

Cavall sat alone in the dark hallway, waiting for Arthur to come back and let him inside. But he didn't. On the other side of the door, the sound of snoring took up a steady tempo. The longer Cavall sat there, the more agitated he became, until he finally stood and began pacing.

He paced and paced and paced and didn't see a single other soul up or down the hall. The only light came from the moon through the windows, casting shadows on the wall. The air was thick from the heat and seemed to muffle even the sound of his toenails clicking on the stones. Occasionally, the hoot of an owl disturbed the stagnant summer's night. Everyone else was asleep.

Cavall's legs were like coiled springs full of energy. It felt like he needed to be ready for something, though he couldn't say what or why. He pawed at the rune stone around his collar. A gift from the Lady of the Lake, it was supposed to warn him of danger, but it wasn't doing anything at the moment. There shouldn't be anything to worry about.

As he rounded a corner, something caught his eye. A faint glow coming from under a door at the end of the hall. So, someone *was* up at this time of night. But he couldn't smell smoke—either from a fireplace or a candle—so what was causing that glow? Curiously, he approached. Soft voices came from within. He perked his ears up and listened.

A woman's voice said, "Did you think I wouldn't notice one of my books missing?"

A man's voice said, "You still don't trust me."

Cavall knew those voices. The woman's voice belonged to Morgana, a witch who lived in the fay woods. Bad things happened when she was around. The man's voice belonged to Morgana and Arthur's son, Mordred. Bad things happened around him, too.

Cavall pressed his nose against the door, and it opened a sliver, enough for him to stick his head inside.

Mordred knelt in the middle of a ring of candles, busily flipping through an enormous book. Even from here, Cavall could smell its pages, ancient and earthy, like something from long ago. Mordred looked up from the book and into a bucket at his side. Cavall cocked his head. That seemed

5

an odd thing to do, let alone in the middle of the night. The contents of the bucket glowed and cast an eerie light all about the room, throwing dark shadows across Mordred's face. His eyebrows knitted together in concentration.

In the far corner, Cavall's brother Glessic lay with his head resting on his front paws. He looked thoroughly bored, but then again, Gless never seemed interested in anything. Not in making friends, not in his own brother, not even in his own person. Not in anything except proving he was better than everyone.

There was no sign of Morgana, but a moment later, her voice echoed from inside the bucket. "What have I told you about fooling with my spell books? Those spells are dangerous, Mordred, even for those who have been trained in the magical arts."

Mordred gritted his teeth. "How do you know I can't do it? You've never even let me try."

"I know which spell you wish to try," Morgana's voice scolded. "No magician has ever successfully performed *that* spell. Even the great wizard Merlin."

"Then perhaps I will be the first."

"Mordred, I'm warning you, as your mother, don't—"

Mordred abruptly stood and kicked the bucket over. Water spilled out onto the floor. The glow vanished, along with Morgana's voice.

"I'll show her," Mordred muttered to himself.

"You should listen to her," Gless said. His voice startled Cavall. He'd almost forgotten his brother was there, and that he could speak to Mordred. The magic that bound him to Mordred as a familiar gave him the ability to do all sorts of things like that. "She knows magic better than you do."

"Not you, too," Mordred said. "You're my familiar. You're supposed to be on my side."

Gless sniffed. "I'm on my own side."

Mordred huffed in disgust and went back to studying the book. "Ungrateful beast."

Cavall wasn't sure what he had just seen, but it made him feel on edge, like his stomach was full of bees. He turned from the door and ran for Arthur's room. He needed to find a way to warn his person that Mordred was using magic in the castle.

As he galloped along, the rune stone on his collar began to vibrate—"singing," the Lady of the Lake had called it. It wasn't a noise, exactly, but a deep rumbling just below the threshold of hearing. Danger was near. Cavall ground to a halt and stood there, his heart beating as rapidly as the stone itself.

A moment later, Cavall caught something move out of the corner of his eye.

He jerked in surprise. Then recovered himself and pointed his nose at where the thing had melted into the other shadows.

"Who's there?" he called.

No response.

The fur on the back of his neck stood on end as he waited for the thing to move again.

As quickly as before, the thing darted from the shadows. This time, Cavall caught sight of it in flashes. It crept along on four legs, the shadow of some beast almost as large as himself, which made it very large indeed. But the strange thing was he couldn't see or smell anything that would cast a shadow like that. It was almost as if the darkness had a mind of its own.

Whatever it was, the persistent buzzing of the stone told Cavall it was dangerous and did not belong in the castle. He lunged at it. It slipped between his paws, as if it weren't even there. Cavall pounced again, and again the shadow glided effortlessly out of his reach. It shot across the hall and slithered like a snake under the doorway to Arthur's room.

Cavall threw himself at the closed door, howling and barking.

"*Now* what?" That was Arthur's voice.

"Go see what the matter is," Gwen's sleepy voice groaned.

The door opened to reveal Arthur, rubbing at his eyes. "What's gotten into you?" he demanded. His harsh tone hurt, but Cavall couldn't tuck his tail in repentance until he'd found that thing.

He pushed his way into the room and sniffed around for any sign of it.

"What are you doink?" Luwella lifted her head from the rug. "Is it not enough that you have woken everyone once already tonight?"

"Where is it?" Frantically, he turned to Arthur, but of

course his person couldn't understand him.

Gwen sat up in bed with a yawn. "What do you suppose—?"

Just then, the shadow creature flitted out from under the bed. Gwen gasped, and Luwella lunged to protect her person—only to crash into the empty wall as the shadow shrank back. It huddled into a shapeless mass, then bolted across the room, up the opposite wall, and under the windowsill, where it disappeared into the darkness outside.

For a long moment, the room seemed frozen in time.

Arthur grabbed the candle from the nightstand. In a flash, time moved again. "What was that?" he asked, running to Gwen's side. "Did you *see* that?"

"I saw it," Gwen answered breathlessly, "but not what it was." She pulled the covers tight around herself. "What if it was a demon?"

"A fay, more like."

"What's the difference?" Gwen asked in a way that suggested she didn't really want an answer. She was not known for her love of the magical beings who lived in the woods beyond the castle. "I've heard of creatures that come in the night. They say it's an old hag who sits on your chest and drains your life force."

"In that case, she's an agile old hag." Arthur laughed, though it failed to lighten the mood.

Cavall looked to Luwella, whose hackles were still raised. "Did *you* see what it was?" he asked.

"Not a what," she answered. "A who. And you know who."

Mordred. Luwella didn't trust Arthur's son either. Could that shadow creature have anything to do with what he'd seen earlier?

Cavall heard Arthur suck in a deep breath. He turned to see his person bending over, casting light from the candle onto the nightstand near his bed. Not more than a foot from where Arthur had been sleeping, four long, deep scratches had been left in the wood.

CHAPTER 2

HE NEXT MORNING, WHEN CAVALL ENTERED
the Round Table room with Arthur, a certain
word lingered on everyone's lips: "assassin."
The knights spoke in angry tones as conversation passed
around the table. The cavernous room echoed with shouts
of disagreement.

Cavall took his usual spot at Arthur's feet. Like the name
suggested, the table was round, so that no one person sat in
the "most important" seat; everyone could address everyone else as equals. And from Cavall's spot beneath the
table, he could see all his fellow dogs among the knights.

Anwen, leader of the hunting dogs, huffed impatiently to herself as she paced back and forth under the table, which she could do with ease given her short legs. Edelm, the oldest and wisest dog Cavall knew, lay at his person's feet, front paws folded in a dignified manner. And . . . Gless, sitting at Mordred's side. Their eyes met for a brief moment, Gless with his usual sneer and challenging gaze.

He and Mordred had something to do with last night. Cavall knew it, with all the fur on his body.

"This is unacceptable," Sir Ector said. He was Arthur's father and Anwen's person, stout, with a bristly bit of hair on his upper lip that made him even look like Anwen a little bit. "How was an assassin allowed to get into the king's room? Where were the guards?"

"Asleep on the job, perhaps," muttered Sir Lancelot, who was Edelm's person. Cavall supposed the person and his dog looked similar in a certain way as well. They both had longish fur . . . or hair, in Lancelot's case, and they both shared the same long, angular face. Even the way they stood was similar, proud and straight and demanding of respect. Cavall had not interacted much with Lancelot, but the knights respected his word, much as Cavall respected Edelm's.

"I think it's more likely," began Sir Bedivere, "that the assassin did not enter through the front gate." Bedivere did not belong to any dog. Nor did his brother, Sir Lucan, who sat next to him at the Round Table. They had the same shade of dark hair, wild and often uncombed.

"Or if they did," Sir Lucan continued as if finishing Bedivere's thought, "it was disguised, so as not to draw attention. Magic, mayhaps."

Cavall didn't know much about the two of them, except that Arthur trusted them enough to make them Knights of the Round Table. But then again, he also trusted Mordred.

Speaking of whom, Mordred was doing an excellent job appearing as enraged as the other knights. "We need to post more guards outside my father's room," he said, slamming his fist on the table. Cavall just knew the shadow creature had something to do with what he'd seen last night in Mordred's room. The other knights believed him, however, and murmured agreement to his proposal. Cavall wished they could understand him. He'd tell them they were being deceived.

"Good idea." Sir Ector spoke again. "I'll have extra guards posted and tell everyone to be watchful for anything suspicious." He stood, pushing his chair back. "In the meantime, perhaps Your Majesty would like to accompany me on a hunt?"

Arthur had been silent since recounting the events of last night. His gaze was far away as he ran his hand absentmindedly through Cavall's fur. He looked up at Ector's words, though.

"Do you think that's wise?" Lancelot said. "It might not be safe."

"Nonsense." Ector waved his hand. "The king needs to get his mind off this matter. And it just so happens there's been a rash of wolves that needs taking care of. I think that would be the perfect thing. Tristan and I will be there, along with half a dozen men. It may very well be safer than staying here, since the assassin expects His Majesty to be in the castle. Besides . . ." He cast kind eyes down at Cavall. "It will be this one's first official hunt. I thought you might like to watch, Your Majesty, seeing as you're so fond of the beast."

Cavall wagged his tail at the praise. A tail was one of the

few ways dogs could make themselves understood to people, and after he'd lost the very end of it, he'd been worried that his would never wag again. Now the mention of his first hunt had it going at full speed.

Anwen said he'd made great progress during training, being able to pick out a specific animal's scent and track it over all types of terrain. But what he was best at was chasing the animal after it had been flushed out. The difficulty was in knowing when to run and when not to. He was learning, though, due in large part to Tristan's patience. Tristan was a good trainer, though Cavall never saw the strange person much outside his training.

Arthur smiled and scratched behind Cavall's ear. "Well, I wouldn't want to disappoint him. A hunt sounds like a fine idea."

Cavall felt an icy pair of eyes on him. He looked up to see Mordred glaring at him.

"If it's not too much to ask, Father, I'd like to come, too." Mordred smiled convincingly. "It's my hound's first hunt as well."

The excitement Cavall had felt a moment ago melted

away. Mordred and Gless would be there, too. Who knew what they were plotting?

To his dismay, Arthur grinned at Mordred's request and clasped his son's hand. "I would be honored to have you join us."

"No." Cavall pawed at Arthur's leg. "Don't let him come. He's going to try to hurt you."

Arthur glanced down at Cavall in confusion. "What is it, boy? What do you want?"

"Perhaps he needs to go out," Mordred said, his voice as slimy as a snake.

Cavall couldn't stand it. He would never be able to do anything as long as Mordred could talk to Arthur and he couldn't. Frustration and helplessness mixed in his gut, until he hopped to his feet and trotted angrily from the meeting hall.

Arthur called after him, but Mordred said, "Let him go, Father. Beasts are so fickle." Cavall didn't know what "fickle" was, but it was probably just another of Mordred's lies.

CHAPTER 3

XCITEMENT HUNG IN THE AIR, AS HEAVY AS the anticipation of a rainstorm.

People chatted with one another on the large field bordering the woods. Horses waited patiently while stable hands checked and double-checked their saddles and reins. Summer insects buzzed in the long grass, while the usual host of small animals hid from the heat of the daytime. The dogs romped around, eager for the chase to begin. Cavall couldn't bring himself to join in, though. Not when Mordred stood right next to Arthur, laughing and cracking jokes with his father as if everything were normal. Gless didn't join in with the other dogs either, but remained by Mordred's side and watched.

"You're looking gloomy, Cavall," Anwen said, waddling up to him on stumpy legs. "I doubt Mordred would try anything with all these people around. And Arthur's got his sword." Cavall was glad to see the magical sword Excalibur on Arthur's belt, even if it was a bit odd, since most of the other people carried javelins or bows and arrows. Only two other people carried swords with them, and Anwen nodded in their direction. "See how Lucan and Bedivere are staying close to him? I bet they're along to protect him in case anything goes wrong."

Cavall had thought it was strange that the two of them would show up, since neither of them had dogs in this hunt. But if they were here to guard Arthur, they weren't doing a very good job by letting Mordred stand so close to him.

"I don't want you distracted on your first hunt." Anwen huffed, causing her jowls to quiver. "We're hunting wolf today, and they can be pretty nasty when cornered."

"Are they tasty?"

"You don't *eat* wolves."

"You don't?" Cavall blinked. "Then why do we hunt them?"

"Because they're menaces. They sneak out of the forest at night and make off with farmers' animals. Sheep, mostly. But they also attack travelers in the woods. Many a person and dog has been hurt or killed by these beasts, so now is not a good time to let your guard down, pup."

Cavall didn't like that. It was bad enough that Mordred and Gless were out to hurt Arthur. Now they were headed into the forest to seek out this dangerous animal.

On the other side of the field, where the tall grass met the forest, two men appeared from out of the trees. Huffing and panting, they made their way to Tristan and pointed in the direction they had come from.

"They've found the wolf," Anwen explained in excitement.

Tristan mounted his horse and blew a single long note on his horn for the dogs to form up. Cavall fell back into his training and rushed to join the other hounds. Maybe Anwen was right. Maybe he should worry less about

Mordred and more about the hunt.

"Starters with me!" Anwen called, and half the dogs, the smaller ones, broke from the group to follow her as she headed into the forest. Arthur, along with perhaps half a dozen other people, mounted his horse and joined the starters, flanked by Bedivere and Lucan on theirs. Cavall knew they should be enough to dissuade Mordred from trying anything, but he still wanted to keep his eyes on his person.

With his long legs, he hurried to catch up to Anwen, bypassing the shorter dogs easily. They were good at chasing over long distances because they kept a steadier pace when running, which meant they didn't tire as quickly, but Cavall was good at short, fast bursts of speed. As he came up behind Anwen, she shot him an annoyed look over her shoulder. "You're not a starting dog, Cavall."

"But—"

"It's *our* job to flush the animal out," she interrupted, deliberately slowing her pace and turning to him. "It's *your* job to chase it once it's out in the open. Or have you really forgotten your training?"

"No, but I—"

"Stick to your task. Who knows, you might even be the one to take the wolf down. That would make your person proud, wouldn't it?"

Cavall shot a concerned look toward Arthur, galloping on his horse toward the woods alongside the starters, mouth wide open in an easy grin. The worry hanging over him since last night had disappeared. He was carefree for the moment, mind on the hunt and not on the creature that had attacked him. "Yes, I guess it would," Cavall admitted.

"I'm glad you understand." She turned to join the other dogs as they passed by, but stopped, as if remembering something. "Don't worry. I'll watch Arthur. You keep an eye on that one." Her eyes rolled toward Mordred, who also remained behind with the finishers. Gless stood by his side, casting suspicious looks at the other dogs.

"I will," Cavall said. "And I'll do my best on the hunt, too."

Anwen nodded her approval. "I'm sure you'll do just fine. Good luck." And with that, she turned and galloped into the forest with the starters.

A man Cavall had sometimes seen in the stables

whistled for the remaining people and dogs to follow him. Mordred mounted his horse, and Gless gave Cavall a dismissive glance before trotting up ahead with him. The brothers had barely spoken since the incident several months ago, when Mordred had drawn his sword on Cavall and his friends and it had become clear that Gless had chosen his person over his brother.

Cavall was nervous as they entered the forest, following a different path from the starters. It seemed he would have more to contend with than just Mordred and Gless. He should have asked more questions. Like how fast wolves were. And how big.

They traveled deep into the forest. In the daylight, it was alive with all sorts of sounds and smells. Birdsong and animal chatter filled the air from above, and from below rose the earthy smell of old leaves and animals that had trod the undergrowth into something resembling a path. Tall, straight trees rose up all around them, and the trails they traveled were covered in fallen leaves that crunched underfoot.

The stable hand found a likely place to corner the wolf

when the hunting party came by. The men dismounted their horses, and everyone settled in to wait.

The sun rose high in the sky. Cavall expected he would hear the barking of dogs and the shouting of men when they were near, but all he heard were the usual daytime sounds of the forest. The men overseeing the finishers talked among themselves. Every so often, one of them would laugh and the others would join in.

The dogs also joined in a group, some stretched out in the sun, others reminiscing about past hunts. The hunt was a social event for people and dogs alike. The horses seemed to want no part of it, as they steadfastly ignored everyone. Likewise, Mordred and Gless had wandered off together on their own. Cavall would feel better having them in sight, but as long as Arthur hadn't arrived yet, they couldn't do much harm, could they?

"Does it usually take this long?" Cavall asked of no one in particular.

"Sometimes a hunt can go on for days," one of the other dogs answered. Cavall couldn't remember her name, but she had shaggy fur that covered her eyes.

"But . . . ," Cavall protested, "we're not supposed to be in the forest after sundown." The fay came out at night, and while he knew that some of the fay were friends and would never hurt them, there were also bad fay to be wary of.

"We won't be here that long," another dog said from the shade of a fallen log. "Not with Tristan leading."

His voice carried such pride that Cavall asked, "Is Tristan your person?"

The dog nodded. He was built like a deerhound, with a big chest, small hips, and long, powerful-looking legs, but he had very short fur and was not nearly as big as Cavall himself. Cavall could not remember seeing him with the other dogs when they had first set out. Where had he come from?

"I taught Tristan everything he knows about hunting," the dog added in a way that wasn't *exactly* bragging but was pretty close.

"You . . . taught Tristan?" Cavall couldn't imagine a dog teaching a person anything. People always just knew more and could do more. Well, perhaps not. After all, Arthur didn't know that Mordred was trying to hurt him, so maybe a dog *could* know more than a person. It still seemed odd to him.

"Drudwyn." The dog with shaggy fur spoke up. "Since the pup's a bit bored, why don't you pass the time by telling us one of your stories?"

"Tell the story of Gelert and Luwellen," one of the other dogs called out.

Cavall wagged his tail. "Yes, please. I'd like to hear."

Drudwyn smiled, almost like a person would. There was something not quite doglike about him. No one spoke as Drudwyn began.

"There once was a prince who lived in these lands named Luwellen the Great, who was a skilled hunter and had a number of hunting hounds. But his favorite was Gelert, and the two of them were rarely seen apart from each other. They hunted together in the high hills and walked along the stony shores of the ocean. Truly, they were the best of friends.

"One day, while out hunting, Gelert had the sudden feeling that something was wrong back at the house with Luwellen's wife and young child. He tried to ignore it, but it was almost like an itch that grows more painful the longer it's ignored. He couldn't shake it. And so he abandoned the hunt and ignored the shouts of his person to come back. He ran as swiftly as the wind travels across the hills until he reached the house. And inside, he found that his fears had been correct.

"While he and Luwellen were gone, a wolf had forced its way into the house. The wife had been struck unconscious, but the wolf was not interested in her. It was trying to attack the child in his crib. Gelert would not allow this to happen, so he lunged at the invader and engaged it in fierce combat. After a brutal fight, Gelert emerged victorious, though badly injured and covered in the wolf's blood. He was about to check the child, for the crib had been knocked over in the fight, but before he could, he heard Luwellen calling him from outside.

"He eagerly ran to meet his person, tail wagging. He knew his person would be pleased with his bravery. However, Luwellen saw only the blood on his teeth and rushed inside, where he found more blood and the upturned crib. 'What have you done?' he cried. 'You have killed my son!'

"Gelert tried desperately to explain what had happened, but Luwellen could not understand him, and, driven mad with grief, he drew his sword and slew Gelert."

"Slew him?" Cavall asked.

"Means 'killed,'" the dog with shaggy fur explained.

"Yes, but—"

"Let Drudwyn finish the story."

"Luwellen," Drudwyn continued, "fell to the floor and wept into his hands for the loss of both his son and best friend. But then he heard a child crying and rushed to the crib. Turning it over, he found his son with a few scrapes and cuts but otherwise unharmed. And next to him lay the dead body of the wolf.

"Realizing what had truly happened, Luwellen was struck anew with grief. He had slain his best friend over a misunderstanding. Heart full of remorse, he carried Gelert's body up the hill they had walked many times and buried him there, honoring his fallen, loyal friend with these words: 'May no man ever lose his friend as I have lost mine. May the power of this prayer bring understanding between beast and man.' And from his eyes fell a single tear, which landed upon Gelert's grave marker and imbued it with this wish.

"It is said that this stone still exists, and that whoever touches it will be granted Gelert's Wish: the power of dogs and people to understand one another."

Drudwyn finished, and Cavall realized he'd forgotten to breathe.

"That's a sad story, Drudwyn," he said.

"It is, if you choose to think of it that way," Drudwyn replied.

Cavall didn't see how you could think of it any other way. A person had killed his best friend over a misunderstanding. Gelert hadn't done anything wrong. Though Luwellen must have felt the way Cavall was feeling now—that Gelert's death had been senseless and tragic.

"Is that a true story?" Cavall asked. "Where did you hear it?"

"It has been passed down from dog to dog and human to human for many, many ages. And I . . ." Drudwyn stretched and yawned. "I am a rememberer of stories."

"Has anyone ever been able to find the stone?"

"There are stories," Drudwyn answered. "Whispers that it rested upon Gelert's grave for many years, but one day was stolen away by a thief and has not been seen since." Drudwyn arched his back and stood. Cavall was surprised to find that he had only one hind leg; the other ended at the thigh. "The hunting party is coming."

Cavall lifted his ears, but he couldn't hear anything. No hoofbeats or voices. The other dogs stood and began to wander back over to the people, so apparently they trusted Drudwyn. Drudwyn himself made his way to the lead man. He had no trouble walking on his three legs.

"The hounds are always the first ones to know, aren't they?" The stable hand laughed, patting Drudwyn's head. He gave a sharp whistle.

As the other men began mounting up their horses, Mordred and Gless stumbled out of the foliage. "What's going on?" Mordred demanded.

"Hunt's on the way," the lead man said from astride his horse. "Better saddle yourself up, lad."

Mordred grumbled darkly under his breath and untied his horse from where he had tethered it to a tree branch.

He was not as quick as the other men to get his foot in the stirrup and climb onto his horse's saddle. The creature gave an indignant snort when Mordred yanked on its reins and spurred its sides. "Watch it, two legs," the horse muttered. Not that Mordred could understand. He only understood Gless.

By the time all the men were on their horses, Cavall could hear the approaching hunt in the distance. The way the horses' hooves beat against the ground sounded like thunder, and it was coming their way.

"Are you ready?" Drudwyn asked, coming up beside him.

"I think so."

"Don't think," Drudwyn reminded him. "You'll do fine. There it is!"

Cavall saw a shape moving through the bushes, headed their way. It didn't smell like anything he'd ever smelled before. Was that the wolf? It looked like a big dog with pointed ears and a shaggy coat. It was covered in mud up to its belly and stumbled as it moved along. It looked exhausted, and suddenly Cavall wasn't so eager to chase it down.

"Now!" Drudwyn barked and the dogs took off, the people following behind. He was fast, and not just for a dog with three legs.

The starter dogs fell away, giving up the hunt to the finishing dogs. Cavall caught sight of Anwen, looking as muddy and worn-out as the wolf. Arthur was there as well. His horse was muddy up to its knees, and he looked tired himself, a sheen of sweat covering his brow. His face was split into a wide grin, even wider when he saw Cavall.

Pride welled up in Cavall's chest and shot out through his tail, making it wag wildly. He would make Arthur proud. He would bring down the wolf so that Arthur could land the finishing blow and become the hero of the hunt. He took off after the other dogs, outstripping them easily with his newfound enthusiasm.

The wolf was up ahead. It smelled like fallen leaves and undergrowth. It smelled like a dog who had never been near people. It was scared, but it was also a proud hunter itself. Cavall could smell all this and more. The distance between them became shorter and shorter. If he could just manage another burst of speed . . .

"Whoa!"

Cavall stumbled when someone yelled behind him. A horse whinnied loudly. Then more yelling.

"Halt!" someone called. "We have a man down!"

Cavall ground to a stop. The wolf slipped away into the woods. Cavall suddenly remembered that he was supposed to be watching Mordred as well. Had he tried to hurt Arthur while Cavall was distracted? From the way the people had stopped to dismount their horses and the worried muttering among them, it sounded like someone had been hurt.

Cavall's heart lurched. Without a second thought, he spun around and raced back toward the people, who had gathered in a circle. He would never forgive himself if Arthur had been hurt.

"Is he badly wounded?" someone asked.

"Calm down, calm down," Tristan's voice said, "let me check on him."

Cavall circled around, sniffing for Arthur. He breathed in relief when he found his person pressed toward the center of the circle. He didn't look or smell hurt, but there was a terrible expression on his face, as if he were in great pain. He held a hand over his mouth as he watched Tristan bend over the figure lying facedown on the forest floor. It was Mordred. He had a large gash on the side of his head.

"What happened?" Bedivere asked. "One minute he was riding beside you and the next . . ."

"His horse threw him," Lucan said. "I saw the whole thing. The boy lost control of the reins."

"He's breathing!" Tristan announced.

Arthur let out a breath. "He's alive."

"But badly hurt," Tristan affirmed. "We need to get him back to the castle right away if he's going to make it."

An icy lump formed in Cavall's stomach as he looked on. It seemed his worries over Mordred might be solved. Then why didn't it *feel* like they were?

CHAPTER 4

HEN THEY RETURNED TO THE CASTLE, THE people carried Mordred upstairs to his room. Cavall followed at Arthur's side. They met Gwen in the hallway, who let out a sharp gasp when she saw Mordred. "What happened?"

"Mordred has been wounded." Arthur placed a hand on her shoulder. "I need to be by my son's side. Would you fetch the physician?"

Gwen nodded and hurried off, with Luwella trailing closely behind her. Cavall noticed that Gless was nowhere in sight.

The men laid Mordred on his bed. He remained unmoving, and his breathing came shallowly. His face was pale.

Arthur sat on the bed and took Mordred's limp hand in his own. "I am sorry, Mordred," he said, which confused Cavall. Arthur hadn't had anything to do with Mordred's fall. "I know I have not always been there for you." He squeezed the hand in his grip, but Mordred did not stir. "But I promise, I am here for you now."

Cavall still didn't understand, but he knew that his person needed comfort. He leaned against Arthur.

Not long after, the castle's physician appeared, flanked by Gwen and Luwella. They waited at the doorway while the physician came in and shooed everyone else away from the bed. "Your Majesty," he said in a slightly scolding tone when Arthur did not immediately step back, "I must have room to work."

Arthur nodded numbly and gave him space, even though it meant leaving Mordred's side. Cavall stayed close by Arthur, and Gwen hugged him tightly.

The physician checked Mordred's wound, felt his neck

and wrists, and then wrapped a bit of cloth that smelled like bitter flowers around the cut on his head. Eventually, he came over to address Arthur and Gwen. "He is in a deep sleep, but his eyes are moving."

"Is that a good sign?" Gwen asked.

"It means he is capable of waking up."

"When?" Arthur asked.

The physician did not respond right away. Even Cavall knew that could not be good.

"I cannot say," he finally said. "I have seen cases like this before. People become . . . trapped in the Dreaming, for lack of a better term. Sometimes it lasts only a short time. Other times it can last for days, even weeks. If that is the case here . . ." He took a deep breath. "I fear Mordred will waste away."

Gwen put a hand to her mouth.

Arthur shook his head. "No, I cannot let that happen. What can we do?"

"Nothing, I am afraid," the physician said. "Only time has the power to cure him now. He will either wake up . . . or he will not."

* * *

By dinnertime, all the dogs had gathered in the great hall to tell the tale of the Hunt That Almost Was, as it had been deemed. "It's lucky we were hunting wolf and not expected to bring back anything to eat," Anwen muttered as the servants brought food in on steaming trays. "Otherwise we would likely all go hungry tonight, thanks to Mordred's accident."

Cavall was only half listening. Mostly he waited for Arthur, who was still upstairs with Mordred. Cavall would gladly be by his side, but the physician had said it was best to keep dogs out of the room.

Eventually, Gwen came down. There was no sign of Arthur. "Your king commands you to eat in his absence," she said as she took her seat at the head of the table. "He wishes to keep vigil over his son."

"Let us pray for the lad," Lancelot said.

"Yes," Gwen agreed stiffly. "Let us pray for his swift recovery." She clasped her hands in front of her, as did the other people.

Cavall didn't feel like talking with the other hunting

dogs, who were still speculating about Mordred's accident. Instead he made his way over to Gless, who sat in the far corner of the dining hall, far from anyone else. Cavall approached slowly, tail down so that Gless would know he wasn't looking for a fight. As he neared, Gless glowered at him. "What do you want?"

Cavall tried to imagine what he would want Gless to say to him if their positions were reversed. He would want some comforting words, just something to let him know that Gless understood what he was going through. "Don't worry," Cavall said at last, "I'm sure your person will be fine."

Gless huffed. "I'm not worried. I'm not like you, Cavall. I don't snivel over my person at every little thing."

Cavall couldn't say whether he sniveled or not, because he wasn't sure what it meant. It sounded like a mean way of saying that he worried about Arthur too much. "You're not afraid Mordred might . . . not wake up?"

"If he doesn't wake up, it means he's weak and that I've chosen the wrong person."

Cavall couldn't imagine feeling that way about Arthur.

It seemed so cold, like Gless didn't really care about his person at all. Maybe he didn't. He didn't seem to care about his own brother. But Mordred had taken care of him, made him his familiar, and kept him by his side. The two of them shared the bond of speech, and yet Gless didn't even care that his person was just barely clinging to life. A bitter part of Cavall thought that Gless didn't deserve a person at all, much less one he could speak with.

Cavall turned back toward the table, where the people ate in uncharacteristic silence. It had been a mistake to comfort Gless. He didn't care about anyone but himself. Even Luwella, who wasn't that friendly to the other dogs, cared about her person. He'd rather have Luwella as company than Gless anyway.

He found her leaning against her person's seat as Gwen ran fingers through her long white fur. "You seem confused," Luwella noted as Cavall flopped down beside her.

"I'm *very* confused," Cavall answered. "I'm not sure how to feel about all of this. Tristan said Mordred might not wake up."

"It would be best if he didn't," Luwella said.

"Yes, I suppose it would."

"You do not sound happy."

"I don't really think it's something to be happy about," Cavall admitted. "I feel bad for Arthur. And . . . I think I feel bad for Mordred, too."

CHAPTER 5

WEN SPENT THE NIGHT IN THE LIBRARY, silently reading from one of her books by the light of a candle, Luwella at her feet. Cavall spent the night with them. No one slept very much.

As the sun broke over the trees, Cavall felt a warm humming against his chest. The rune stone. But this wasn't the usual reaction it had to danger. In fact, the only time he'd seen it do this had been around . . .

He jumped to his feet and ran to the window. Startled, Gwen dropped her book. "What is it?" She and Luwella joined him, peering out to the road leading up to the castle, and the bent figure making its way slowly up the road. "Merlin," Gwen breathed.

Cavall was glad to see the wizard, who had always been kind and patient with him and who, as a fay, knew how to listen to what dogs were saying. Cavall kept close by Gwen's side as she ran down to greet him, still in her night-gown and wrapped in a thick robe.

"Arthur needs your help," she explained as she led the way to Mordred's room.

"Yes, I know," Merlin said. "I came as soon as I heard."

"How did you hear?" Gwen asked.

"The forest speaks to me, and it told me of the accident. Though there is word that it was no accident."

"No accident? You mean someone planned for Mordred to fall from his horse?"

Merlin didn't answer that. It could be aggravating at times, how he didn't always explain things clearly. He always seemed to know more than he let on.

He walked heavily with his staff and so slowly that Gwen often needed to slow her pace to not get too far ahead. When they reached Mordred's room, she held the door open for the old man. Merlin smiled in appreciation.

Arthur had pulled a chair up next to Mordred's bed and fallen asleep leaning heavily forward on the mattress, head cradled in his arms. "Arthur, husband," Gwen called in a soft voice that nonetheless caused him to bolt upright. He looked around, as if he didn't remember where he was. Then his face contorted when he saw Mordred lying before him.

Cavall whined to see his person in such distress and came over to nudge his head under Arthur's arm. The look on Arthur's face faded just slightly, and he ran his fingers through the fur on Cavall's neck.

Merlin came around to the other side of the bed and laid a hand on Mordred's forehead.

Arthur watched him intently. "Can you do something for him? Some magic?"

Merlin shook his head sadly. "You know my magic cannot do such things."

"But there must be something . . ." He trailed off. The hand petting Cavall's neck went slack as Arthur sank back into the chair. Cavall had seen that look on his face before, when he'd entered the Dreaming to fight off the Night Mare that had been plaguing Arthur's mind. It was a look of defeat and hopelessness.

Merlin was silent for a while. His bushy eyebrows, white with age, drew together as he thought. "Loki . . ." He pinched the bridge of his nose.

Arthur sat up straight. "Loki? What is Loki?"

Merlin took a deep, aggravated breath. Cavall had never seen him look annoyed before, the way Gless did when Cavall said or did something stupid. "Tell me," he said at last, "what have you heard of the Holy Grail?"

Gwen gasped. "The cup that has power to heal any affliction or wound? That is an old fay tale." She must have realized that she was speaking to a fay, because she quickly added, "Begging your pardon. My books say it is a myth."

Arthur looked from Gwen to Merlin. "A cup that can heal?" he repeated.

"The Grail is no myth," Merlin continued. "Whoever drinks from it will find themselves cured, even of deadly wounds. Though I have not seen it with my own eyes, I know those who have."

Arthur stood, the look of defeat gone from his face, replaced with a shining hopefulness. Cavall's tail thumped against the stone floor. "Where would I find such a thing?"

"Ah, therein lies the problem." Merlin tapped the side of his nose. "It was lost to the ages. It was once in the possession of a powerful fay called the Fisher King, but it was stolen from his court many, many years ago. It remains lost to this day."

"Does nobody know where to find it?" Arthur pressed.

Merlin took in a deep breath, as if considering what to say next.

Cavall knew what he wanted to say, though. If he could say it directly to Arthur, he would. "Merlin," he said, "I know Arthur wants to save Mordred, but he shouldn't. Mordred just wants to hurt him, maybe even kill him. Can you tell him that?"

Merlin stared intently at Mordred on the bed, unmoving. After a moment, he sighed. "Arthur, your intentions are good," he began slowly, with a voice full of age, "but there are some who say Mordred is not worth saving."

"Who?" Arthur's fists clenched. "Who would say such a

thing? I'll take the head from his shoulders."

Cavall flinched at the reaction.

"There is no one who is not worth saving," Arthur continued as his hands uncurled. The anger left his voice, replaced by sadness and regret. "I know my son has not made the best impression at Camelot, but I take the blame for that upon myself. The boy deserves a chance to prove himself, and I . . . I hope that I deserve another chance to teach him how to be a good man." He bowed his head in a silent plea. "Please, Merlin, if you know how to find the Holy Grail, I beseech you, tell me. I will do whatever you ask of me in return."

Cavall looked from one to the other. Arthur wore his pain so clearly on his face, it made Cavall hurt for him.

At last, Merlin waved his hand. "Enough, King Arthur. You do not bow to me. We are friends, you and I, equals. I will help you find the Holy Grail, and in return, you must promise to use the power of the Grail wisely. That is all I ask."

"Yes, of course." Arthur raised his head. "I promise it, Merlin. I promise it."

"The fay who stole the Grail was a trickster, a mischievous spirit who delighted in . . . shall we say, parting valuables and their owners. It is said he has a cave full of mysterious wonders from all over the world, well hidden and guarded by a fierce beast."

Gwen's hand went to her throat in alarm. "What manner of beast?"

Cavall didn't like the sound of that either.

"It doesn't matter," Arthur announced, so loudly that Cavall jumped. "Whatever beast it is, I will slay it. I am not afraid."

"No." Gwen put a hand on his shoulder. "Be afraid, husband. If you will not think of your own life, then think of what will become of me if you are not careful. Think of what will become of Mordred if he should wake to find his father has been slain on his account."

Arthur relaxed his shoulders. "You're right, Gwen." He blushed, looking ashamed at his momentary foolhardiness. "Of course you're right. I mustn't be rash. I will inform the knights and . . ." His eyes widened. "I shall make a quest of it. A quest for the Holy Grail."

"No," Cavall cried, but it only came out as a bark. "Don't go on a dangerous quest on Mordred's account."

But Arthur had a determined glint in his eye. He turned to Merlin. "How do I find this cave?"

Merlin rested his knobby-fingered hand against Cavall's head. "Cavall will show you the way."

Cavall lifted his head in surprise. "Me? But I don't know where the Holy Grail is."

Merlin bent just enough to grasp the rune on Cavall's collar. "This," he said, rubbing the stone between his fingers, "will tell you when you are near."

"I thought it only made noise when danger was near." And around you, he thought, but wasn't sure if that was rude to say.

"This rune represents guidance and truth," Merlin said, indicating the symbol engraved on the stone. "It is the language of the old fay and was created with very old magic. To those who listen, it warns of danger, but it can also guide you." His face became wistful as he studied the rune. "The fay who stole the Holy Grail from the Fisher King was powerful, and traces of him still remain, though he has long since left this land. This stone will react when his artifacts are near. Listen to it. Follow it."

"I will," Cavall promised in a bark that startled both Arthur and Gwen, who had been watching them speak with odd expressions on their faces. It must be odd to them, since they could not understand dogs, to hear a one-sided conversation.

Merlin released the rune and stood to his full height, stooped though it was. "Cavall has vowed to lead you to the Holy Grail," he announced to the people.

Arthur's face split into a broad grin. "I trust he will."

Cavall's tail wagged wildly to know that his person believed in him.

Arthur bolted upright. "I am going on a quest. I must tell everyone immediately."

And with that, he spun around and ran from the room.

For a moment, Gwen, Cavall, and Merlin stood looking at one another, then they hurried after him.

Gwen slowed her pace to help Merlin, but Cavall ran ahead. He caught up to Arthur on the winding staircase that led down to the great hall. The smell of warm, yeasty food drifted upward, carried by the noise of breakfasters clinking plates and sharing conversation. Everything fell silent as Arthur burst through the doors. Gless, sitting next to Mordred's empty chair, raised his head, an expectant look on his face.

"I am going on a quest," Arthur announced. His voice filled the large hall. "A quest to find the Fisher King's Holy Grail. I must ride quickly if I am to save my son's life, so I may only take a handful of men with me. Our journey will be perilous and fraught with dangers. Do not take this request lightly. My friends, which of you will join me?"

A single moment of silence followed as his words took meaning.

Sir Ector was the first on his feet. "I will go, my king," he announced.

Arthur smiled and came around the table to clasp Ector on the shoulder. "I thank you for your offer, Father," he said, "but you are the closest thing Mordred has to family after me. I would feel better knowing you were here looking after him."

Ector set his mouth in a tight, straight line, like he wanted to argue, but instead he nodded. "I will," he said. "I promise. But will you at least bring Anwen in my stead?

Her nose is unrivaled, and *I* would feel better knowing you had her with you."

Arthur smiled warmly. "It is no small thing to entrust another man with one's dog. I am honored."

"I will go," Sir Lucan announced. "I am the best rider, and your bodyguard besides."

"And wherever my brother goes, so do I," Sir Bedivere added. "We will gladly lend you our swords, just as we did at the Battle of Bedegraine, where we both fought in your name, not only as the rightful king of England but also as our friend."

Arthur looked from one brother to the other. "I trust you with my life," he said. "Both of you. I accept your pledge. Make your arrangements. We leave with all haste."

A trumpet blared, trying desperately to sound triumphant on this particularly bleak day. The entire castle came to see them off. A sea of flags flapped in the wind, as if trying to break free from their poles. Clouds hung low and dark in the sky. Rain threatened to fall at any moment. It was not a good day to be out of the castle.

"Bad day to start a quest," Anwen said. Her long ears

caught a gust of wind and flew back against her head.

Amid the banners, Arthur waved to the crowd, and the crowd cheered back. Arthur and his knights looked commanding in their armor—knee-length tunics over shirts made of rings of metal. Cavall thought it very odd, but he understood it was meant for protection. Just like the swords strapped to their belts. Everything else looked to be for show. Even the horses were dressed, with clothes that looked like skirts draped over their backs and rumps.

Gwen's dress blew and snapped in the wind, but she stood as strong and commanding as Arthur did in his armor. She had a worried look about her as she cupped his face in her hands. "Are you sure you will not rethink this? You are still tired from watching over Mordred all night. You might wait another day."

Arthur shook his head and placed his own hands over hers. "Time is of the essence. Mordred does not have long, and I cannot delay."

"I feel better knowing you have Cavall and the others at your side," Gwen said hesitantly. "But I will still worry for you, husband."

He drew her close and wrapped his arms around her for

a long time. Arthur eventually broke away. He ran a hand through Gwen's wind-tossed hair. "I will hurry home. Take care of Mordred for me."

Her face hardened with resolve, and though Cavall knew she did not trust Mordred, she didn't hesitate to answer. "I will."

They kissed, then Arthur mounted his horse. Bedivere and Lucan sat astride theirs already, while the horses pawed impatiently at the dirt.

"Wait!" someone barked, and then the crowd parted as a figure made its way between the people's feet. "I'm coming, too."

Cavall blinked, then shook his head and blinked again, just to make sure he wasn't seeing things. Gless appeared from out of the crowd, panting and out of breath. He composed himself quickly, though, and butted his way between Cavall and Anwen.

"I said, I'm coming, too."

Anwen narrowed her eyes at him. "Why?"

"Because I'm the fastest, strongest, smartest dog in Camelot, and you'll be able to find the Holy Grail much more quickly with my help."

That didn't sound like Gless at all. Well, the fastest, strongest, smartest part, yes, but . . .

"Why do you want to find the Holy Grail so badly?" Cavall asked.

Gless snorted and turned his head away. "I cannot stand the thought that others will say my fool of a brother and his foolish friends found such a rare and precious artifact, while Gless, who is clearly superior, did not."

"Brat," Anwen huffed. "*I'm* still the pack leader. *I* still get the final say in who comes or not, and there's no way we're letting *you* come on this quest with us."

"Anwen, wait." Cavall took a careful step toward his brother. "Gless, do you want to come because you're worried about Mordred?"

"No, of course not."

Cavall tried to catch his brother's eyes, but Gless would not look at him.

"Anwen, I think we should let him come, too."

Gless did look up at that, a surprised expression on his face.

"You do?" Anwen asked in shock.

"He's right. He is faster, stronger, and smarter—than

me at least!" he added quickly. "Maybe we will find it faster with his help. But only . . ." Cavall hardened his face to show he was serious. "If you promise not to try anything sneaky. No trying to hurt Arthur or anyone else."

"I—"

"And," Anwen interrupted him, "no running off on your own. And you have to recognize that *I'm* the pack leader, and that means you do what I say."

Gless bristled. "Fine," he muttered. "I promise."

Anwen glared at him. "All right," she said at last. "You can come. But I'm keeping my eyes on you."

A horse nickered and drew their attention back to Arthur and the knights, who had brought their horses around and stood poised under the archway that led out to the road. The dogs ran to catch up with them.

"Ah, Gless," Arthur said, "I see you're joining us as well."

Cavall hoped he hadn't made a mistake in letting Gless come.

"Take care," Arthur said to the gathered crowd, lifting a hand to wave them farewell. "When we return, we will have the Holy Grail."

CHAPTER 6

THEY HAD ONLY BEEN TRAVELING FOR ABOUT an hour when the overcast morning gave way to rain. The dirt road turned to mud, and everyone was miserable, plodding along up to their ankles in muck—or up to their chests, in Anwen's case.

The horses kept a steady pace, occasionally flicking droplets from their ears and manes. Cavall's and Gless's wiry coats kept them from getting too wet, but Anwen was soon soaked. The people didn't fare much better, since their metal armor was not meant for comfort. Although people used armor to protect themselves against their enemies' weapons, Cavall wondered if they didn't also use it to make themselves appear bigger, the way barn cats puffed out their fur when anyone came too near them.

Even though they'd left the castle some time ago, it still felt as if someone was watching them from afar. Someone who didn't wish them well on their journey. Cavall hadn't felt anything from the stone yet—either danger or old fay magic—but the road was long and so far only went in one direction. He hoped the stone would tell him when to turn.

As Cavall walked along, taking care not to get his big paws stuck in the mud, he became aware of someone walking beside him—someone taller than Anwen but shorter than Gless. He looked over.

"Drudwyn?"

The strange storytelling dog smiled at him. It was just as unnerving as it had been the day of the hunt. "Hello again, Cavall."

"Where . . . ?" Cavall looked over his shoulder, as if that would tell him where Drudwyn had appeared from. Could it have been Drudwyn watching them? Probably not, because it still felt like someone—or some*thing*—was watching them. With displeasure. "What are you doing here?"

On Cavall's other side, Gless huffed. "I hope you're not planning on coming, too, three legs," he grumbled. "You'll only slow us down."

Cavall felt embarrassed at his brother's words. Drudwyn didn't deserve to be insulted like that. And he wasn't slowing them down. He didn't even stumble at all in the deep mud like the rest of them. If he was insulted, though, he didn't show it. "I just thought I'd see you off," he said. "I heard you were looking for the Holy Grail."

Suddenly, Cavall was even gladder to have him there. "Drudwyn," he said, "do you know any stories about the Holy Grail or the monster that guards the cave Merlin told us about?"

"Hmm . . ." Drudwyn paused to think. "No stories, as such. Stories have a beginning and an ending, and I've heard only bits and pieces here and there."

"What have you heard?"

They sloshed through a puddle. Anwen disappeared

up to her neck, but Drudwyn waded through as if it were nothing.

"The guardian of the cave," Drudwyn began, "is a monstrous wolf, so large that it can see over treetops. Legend has it that the creature is the familiar of a great magician who collected treasures from all over the world and hoarded them in the cave for himself. The magician eventually disappeared—either died or left for further adventures—but his familiar remained, guarding its master's treasures through the ages."

"Who was this magician?" Gless asked skeptically.

"Oh, he has many names. Lie-Smith, Silver Tongue, Skywalker, Wolf Father. But most know him as Loki."

Loki. That was the name Merlin had muttered earlier. Cavall noted it but did not interrupt.

"There are many stories of his mischief," Drudwyn went on. "But concerning the Holy Grail, it is said he betrayed the Fisher King, stealing his most prized possession and mortally wounding him in the process. Though the Lie-Smith is a liar by nature, so it's difficult to tell truth from fabrication." His eyes twinkled. "We storytellers are not too concerned with that."

Gless wrinkled his nose in distaste. "You speak in riddles. You're no help."

"I like your stories," Cavall offered.

Drudwyn smiled. "There is something else I've heard about the cave that might interest you."

"Yes?"

"Do you remember the story of Luwellen and Gelert? How the stone that contained Luwellen's wish was stolen from Gelert's grave?"

Cavall nodded. He wouldn't forget that story any time soon.

"There are some who note that Loki was wreaking all manner of mischief across these lands just about the time the Wish went missing."

"Are you suggesting," Anwen snorted, emerging from a mud puddle, "that the thief is actually this Loki character?"

"I am merely suggesting what was suggested to me."

Cavall's heart picked up a pace. "Are you sure?"

Drudwyn tilted his head from side to side. "I'm sure I heard stories, yes."

"No help at all," Gless muttered.

"Thank you for telling me," Cavall said. "If Gelert's Wish is in this cave, then I'll find it, and use it to talk to Arthur." And tell him about Mordred, Cavall thought, though he probably shouldn't say that with Gless around.

Up ahead, Arthur pulled his horse to a stop. They'd reached a fork in the road. Off to the right were more fields and flat lands. To the left, about a mile or so down, the path led into the forest.

"Which way?" Bedivere asked, looking both ways.

Cavall looked first down one path, then the other. He had never been this far from the castle, from home. Both roads seemed equally terrifying and unknown. And yet he was expected to know which one would lead to the Holy Grail. For the first time, it struck him, the true responsibility he'd taken when agreeing to this quest. Everyone was depending on him.

He stood very still and tried to block out the sounds around him: the people's voices, the thrum of the rain, even his own doubts. Merlin had said the rune would react, different than if there were danger. And there it was. Not a noise, exactly, but a faint, rhythmic pulsing. Like a heartbeat.

He took a step to the right. The pulse faded.

He took a step to the left. The pulse increased, ever so slightly, and the rune grew warmer against his throat.

Cavall barked and pointed with his nose down the road leading to the forest.

"Looks like you have your answer, Bedivere." Arthur laughed. It was good to hear him laugh. From atop his horse, he looked down and gave Cavall a knowing wink. "I never doubted you, boy."

Cavall wagged his tail at the praise. He had not let his person down.

"Perhaps we should break for the night," Lucan suggested. "There's only an hour or so of traveling light left."

"That's an hour or so we should spend on the road," Arthur said, spurring his horse onward.

"But . . . Your Majesty," Bedivere called after Arthur, "that will leave us in the middle of the forest at night."

"We will be fine as long as we stay on the path," Arthur called over his shoulder. He didn't slow down, and he was quickly leaving them all behind. Cavall ran to catch up, and this prompted the others to follow as well.

"This is where I leave you!" Drudwyn called after them.

"Good luck on your travels, friends!"

"Thank you," Cavall called back. "For everything."

They trotted down the road at a brisk pace, until the rolling fields were behind them and the forest loomed ahead. The party plunged onward, even Bedivere and Lucan, who Cavall saw exchange brief, uncertain glances.

It was less windy and rainy on the other side, since it was more shielded from the storm, but a few raindrops still managed to make it through the treetops. The sound of rain against the leaves was like the skittering of hundreds of tiny paws. Some birds chirped, but every other creature was quiet, probably sheltering somewhere safe. Perhaps the rain would keep any unfriendly fay at bay as well.

The road was wide and easy to follow, so Arthur could be right. If they stayed on the road and didn't stray too far off it, maybe the fay would not think of it as trespassing.

Among the bushes, something moved, and Cavall turned quickly to see.

"What is it?" Anwen asked, seeing that he had stopped.

Cavall scanned the trees with his eyes, relying on the sight deerhounds were known for. And Cavall had extraordinary eyes for a dog—he could even see the color blue. But now, no matter how hard he looked, he couldn't make out anything. He could have sworn he saw something about the size and shape of a dog, but there was no sign of such a creature.

The rune stone on his collar was not singing at any danger. So Cavall told himself that it meant them no harm. Either that or he was imagining things.

CHAPTER 7

HEY FOLLOWED THE SOGGY ROAD UNTIL IT WAS too dark for the people to see. Cavall could still find his way by scent, but he was relieved when Arthur gave them the go-ahead to make camp. He was tired, and from the way Arthur moved stiffly as he dismounted his horse, it seemed he was tired as well. They all were.

"Just remember to stay on the path," Arthur said. "And no fire. We should be fine, but that doesn't mean we want to announce our presence either."

"Too wet for a fire anyway," Bedivere said as he unpacked

66

his bedroll and spread it out on the ground in the cover of a willow tree, where the rain did not penetrate through the leafy branches so much.

"I'll take the first watch," Lucan announced. "You look like you could use some sleep, Your Majesty."

Arthur nodded with a grateful smile on his face. "Thank you, Lucan. And Bedivere, for accompanying me on this journey. Neither of you needs to call me 'Your Majesty' while we're together. Arthur is fine."

He unrolled his own bedroll next to Bedivere's and put one of the extra packs out for a pillow. Cavall padded over and leaned against him. He couldn't do anything about the rain, but he could at least try to keep his person warm. Arthur roughed the fur on Cavall's back, then reached into the pack and pulled out some dried meat, which he broke in two. Half for himself and half for Cavall. Cavall ate his bit quickly. It was tough and salty and satisfying when everything around him was wet and miserable. If quests meant getting food like this every day, maybe they weren't so bad.

Bedivere fed Anwen and Lucan fed Gless from their own

provisions. Gless took his dinner and retreated to the edge of the camp. Anwen, however, curled up next to Bedivere, who laughed. "Perhaps I will end up stealing Ector's dog."

"Maybe you should think about getting a dog yourself," Lucan offered as he double-checked the ropes tied loosely around the horse's hooves to make sure they wouldn't run off in the middle of the night. Horses would wander if left to their own devices.

"I've never found one that suits me," Bedivere said.

"Perhaps a deerhound is what you need," Arthur suggested. He climbed into his bed, and Cavall lay down, pressing as close to Arthur's body as possible. Back at the castle, Gwen never allowed him up on the bed, so being close to his person like this was pleasant. This quest stuff wasn't turning out so bad after all. "I'll speak with the kennel master about getting a pup for you."

"Thank you, Your— Arthur. I must admit, Cavall is a fine hound, as are Anwen and . . ." Bedivere hesitated and shot an uncertain look at Gless. "Gless is the perfect hound for Mordred. But as for me . . . I don't know how to put it. No dog I've met has fit my personality so well. I envy the bond you share with your beast, but I believe it's something that must happen on its own. I know I'll have found the right one when I meet it."

"Isn't that what you say about women?" Lucan chuckled.

Bedivere picked up a small pebble and lodged it at Lucan. It bounced harmlessly off his armor, which he had not taken off yet. "Quiet, you. Your king can't possibly sleep with all the jabbering you're doing."

"Oh, I'm the one jabbering?" Lucan continued with that same amused tone.

"Enough, the two of you," Arthur said gently. "We have another long day of traveling ahead of us tomorrow. I suggest we get some rest."

"I'll take second watch," Bedivere said. "You should have as much uninterrupted sleep as you can, Y . . . Arthur."

Arthur and Bedivere settled in. Their breathing evened out as they fell asleep, and even Anwen was snoring within minutes.

As Cavall himself began to drift toward sleep, he noticed Gless had not lain down yet. He remained awake with Lucan, though it didn't look like he was really keeping watch. He stood far away from the person, not even scanning the forest for danger. Rather, he had his nose pointed downward, at a large puddle that had formed in the rain. He seemed to be . . . muttering at it? Cavall wasn't sure what to make of that. Maybe he should ask? But no sooner had he considered the possibility than sleep began to pull heavily at his eyelids. It had been a long day.

He laid his head on Arthur's chest. The steady rise and fall was comforting, and soon he found himself drifting off to sleep as well.

Cavall awoke to the sound of squelching footsteps through wet leaves. He lifted his head to look around in the dark.

Arthur was still asleep. In fact, he hadn't moved even an inch. The horses were silent and shifted uncertainly in their hobbles. Something had spooked them.

Bedivere and Lucan were nowhere in sight. Then Cavall noticed Anwen and Gless standing at the edge of the camp, staring into the forest. It was odd to see them standing together, not going after each other. Cavall made his way over to them. "What's wrong?"

"Noise coming from in there," Anwen said.

"It sounded like a wounded beast," Gless added.

"Lucan went to check it out," Anwen explained. "Bedivere told him not to go, but he was insistent. They both went into the forest a few moments ago. Wasn't sure if we should follow them or not."

"I'm not chasing after some foolhardy humans," Gless said. "If they end up dead, it's their own fault."

Anwen curled her lip at him. "I would've gone after, but I didn't know if I should leave you and Arthur unguarded."

Gless snorted. "I told you I had no intention of hurting Arthur, didn't I?"

"Even if I took your word for it," Anwen snarled, "there's still some shadowy thing that went after the king a few nights ago."

Yes, there was that as well.

"I'll go," Cavall said, trotting past them. "Anwen, you stay here and watch Arthur. Gless, call if they come back."

Anwen and Gless shared a spiteful glance at each other before nodding. "All right."

The rain had picked up during the night, but that made it easier to track Lucan's and Bedivere's scents through the undergrowth. He could also hear the noise Gless had mentioned. It did sound like a wounded animal . . . a wounded dog almost: a soft whimpering, broken every so often by a low growl. The rune stone on Cavall's collar made an odd noise as well. It started to sing as if there was danger nearby, then faded into a soft hum. Then it sang again. What could that mean? Was someone hurt out there who needed help?

He followed Bedivere's and Lucan's muddy footprints until he could hear the two knights whispering to each other.

"Leave it, Lucan. We shouldn't be off the road."

"I just need to see."

"Whatever it is, it's nothing good. It's probably a fay trying to lure us away."

"Then go back."

"And leave my brother to certain doom? What would Mother say?"

"She'd say it was very shocking because you were always the reckless one."

"I'm not reckless."

"Of course you are."

"I am n— Gaah!" Bedivere shrieked as Cavall nudged him from behind.

Lucan spun. He held a knife in his hand, but quickly lowered it when he recognized Cavall. Then he burst out laughing.

"Would you be quiet?" Bedivere hissed. "You'll bring every fay in the forest down on us."

"Not if your screaming didn't do it first." Lucan patted Cavall's head. "You about startled us to death there." He chuckled.

Cavall tucked his tail between his legs to show he was sorry.

A long, mournful howl broke through the rain. Lucan turned, knife in hand, and began creeping forward. Bedivere looked like he wanted to keep arguing, but instead he followed after, muttering darkly to himself and shooting disapproving looks at Cavall.

The whimpering grew louder and more panicked as they got closer. Cavall could smell the animal through the rain. It smelled familiar, almost like a—

"Wolf!" Bedivere cried.

He and Lucan ducked behind some ferns, and Cavall joined them. Together, they all peered at the wolf struggling in a trap. One of her hind legs was snared by a thick twine rope as she jerked her body to and fro, trying to get loose.

"Local farmer must have set the trap," Bedivere said. He winced as the wolf gave a sharp tug on her trapped leg that made her howl in pain. "Might as well put the poor thing out of its misery."

"I'll do it," Lucan said, treading forward with his knife raised.

"You might want to use your sword," Bedivere called after him. "Longer reach."

"I know what I'm doing."

The wolf stilled as Lucan approached. She was a bit smaller than Cavall, and her fur was thicker than any dog's Cavall had seen. She bared her teeth at Lucan. A warning growl rumbled from her throat. The rune stone began to sing.

"Easy." Lucan held up his free hand. "I'm not going to hurt you."

He wasn't? Then why was he still holding his knife?

Cavall got his answer when Lucan knelt down and reached for the rope holding the wolf's paw. Cavall saw Lucan's intent, but apparently the wolf did not because she whirled around and snapped at him with her teeth. The rune stone shrieked.

"Lucan!"

Lucan nodded to Bedivere to show he was unhurt and turned back to the wolf. "Easy there," he said. "Easy, girl." Slowly, he reached out again.

The rune stone faded to a gentle hum again. The wolf watched distrustfully but didn't snap at him as he took hold of the rope. She did panic when he raised his knife. She whimpered and pulled at her bonds so hard that Lucan was having trouble cutting the rope.

"Lucan, don't," Bedivere said. "Kill it and be done."

Lucan ignored him and began sawing at the rope with the knife. The wolf's thrashing made it difficult.

"Don't struggle!" Cavall barked. "He's trying to help you."

The wolf's head swung toward him. As their eyes met, Cavall noted a tuft of white fur on her forehead. In her surprise, she stopped fighting, and Lucan finally severed the rope with a *twang*. He gave a cry of triumph as the wolf pulled free.

She darted into the bushes, pausing just long enough to shoot a questioning look over her shoulder. Then she was gone.

"I'm sure it appreciated that," Bedivere said, coming out from behind the ferns. Cavall followed. "The farmer who set the trap, on the other hand, will have you to blame if his sheep go missing."

Lucan tucked his knife away with a guilty grin. "Didn't seem sporting to kill her while she was so vulnerable. Tristan's always going on about how you have to be sporting when hunting."

Bedivere shook his head. "I'm not much for hunting, myself. Only went on Tristan's last hunt to protect Arthur. Speaking of whom . . ."

"Right, right." Lucan stood. "We should get back to camp before we're missed."

Bedivere clapped his brother on the shoulder. "Let's hope that's the last of that wolf we'll be seeing. It looked like it'd been in that trap for a day or two, so it might be pretty hungry."

"Yes, well . . ." Lucan wiped the rain from his eyes. "I guess I've always had a soft spot for the animal that shares my name."

CHAPTER 8

THE RAIN STOPPED AT ABOUT THE TIME ARTHUR got up for his watch shift. Cavall stayed by his side the rest of the night, worrying what would happen if the wolf came back. But dawn broke through the trees with no sign of her.

They sat together, watching the sun cast long shadows across the forest floor. Everyone else was asleep. It was still and peaceful. Arthur remained silent. His mind seemed far away as he ran his hand absently over Cavall's head and neck.

Cavall wanted to say something. Something that would

make Arthur smile or laugh, or at least something that would ease his mind. They sat so close together, and yet it felt as if a vast chasm kept them apart. Cavall leaned over and licked Arthur's face.

Arthur sputtered in surprise, wiped his face, and then laughed. "I suppose it's time to wake the others," he said, standing.

The men ate breakfast from their packs and fed the dogs and horses. Cavall got another piece of dried meat and a bit of bread. Armor went back on and packs were reloaded onto the horses.

As they set out, Cavall took the lead, at each twist in the path going where the rune stone told him. Although the telltale "singing" that indicated danger never sounded, Cavall couldn't shake the feeling that someone was watching them from the trees, the same as yesterday.

They traveled straight along the road for most of the morning, until the rune's beat abruptly faded. Cavall stopped short, and so did Anwen behind him. Even Gless looked up from his place in back.

"What's wrong?" Lucan asked. "What's he—?"

"Shh." Bedivere put a finger to his lips and urged them to be silent.

Cavall backtracked a few steps and, yes, the beat picked up. A smaller path branched off in that direction, really no more than a trail wide enough for one horse at a time. He walked a few paces down that way, and the beat became faster again. He looked over his shoulder to the others.

"That way it is, then," Arthur announced. He steered his horse onto the trail. Lucan and Bedivere followed single file behind him. The dogs trotted on and off the path, ducking around trees and bushes as they went.

"I don't suppose," Bedivere said, "that the fay will leave us alone again tonight if we agree to stay on this path."

"We'll need to be extra alert," Arthur answered.

Now that the rain had passed, the forest was once again alive with sounds. Squirrels jumped from branch to branch, causing the trees to sway. Rabbits darted into the bushes. Every time Cavall caught a hint of them, whether it was a smell, a noise, or a quick movement out of the corner of his eye, he had to force himself not to run after them. He needed to remain focused.

Arthur rode with grim determination. Cavall should mimic him, not get distracted from their quest. Of course, Arthur wanted to find the Holy Grail, but all Cavall could think of was finding Gelert's Wish. Did that make him a bad dog? It felt like he wasn't really doing this to help his person. Or if he was, it was more so that he could help himself. But no—he wanted to find Gelert's Wish to warn Arthur not to trust Mordred. That was a good thing.

No matter how much he turned it around and around in his mind, it still felt like he was lying to Arthur. And it felt like he was lying to himself, as well.

They had a good pace going when, suddenly, Anwen stopped in her tracks.

Cavall and Gless looked back at her. "What is it?" Cavall asked.

Anwen furrowed her brow, eyes trained on something in the drying mud. Cavall trotted up to see. It was a paw print, almost as big as his own, but not in a place he had been walking. Anwen set her nose on the ground and sniffed it.

"What's wrong?" Cavall asked again.

"Smell this print," Anwen instructed. "What do you notice?"

Gless sniffed, then Cavall.

"Nothing," Cavall answered. He was confused. What was he supposed to be smelling for?

"Exactly," Anwen said with a nod. "I thought this might be one of your paw prints at first, but it doesn't smell like either of you. It doesn't smell like anything. Doesn't that seem odd?"

Gless studied the print. "Could the rain have washed it out?"

"Whatever made these tracks," Anwen said, "it came by this way recently. The print is new, definitely after the rain stopped." She looked one way, then the other, as if searching for something. But nothing appeared amiss. At night, when the fay were up and about, the forest tended to . . . shift and change, and things were not as they seemed. But during the day, it was just a peaceful forest. Sunlight filtered in through the branches, chasing the damp from last night's rain. The most menacing noise was the chirping of birds overhead. "We should keep our eyes open."

They trudged on, keeping their eyes, ears, and noses alert for anything strange. Cavall couldn't help but think about the wolf Lucan had set free last night. He hoped the knight's decision wouldn't come back to bite them. Literally.

They rode all morning and broke for lunch when the shadows began to change angles, becoming longer and more pronounced. They found a clearing near a brook, with plenty of shade from low-hanging tree branches. The night had been cold, but the day was sweltering, and it felt good to drink deeply from the crystal waters while the people refilled their water skins.

After drinking his fill, Cavall lay down on the mossy bank in the cool shade. A breeze picked up, rustling the leaves. The sound lulled him. He had to admit, he was tired. He hadn't gotten much sleep last night, with the wolf incident and then staying awake for Arthur's watch as well.

Perhaps a few minutes of rest would be all right. He allowed his eyes to close as he thought of what he would do once he found Gelert's Wish.

What would he say to Arthur? Obviously he would warn him about Mordred and tell him not to risk his life to save someone who only wanted to hurt him. But what about after that?

He'd thank his person, first of all, for choosing him and never giving up on him, even when he made mistakes. He'd thank Arthur for trusting him enough to hunt with the other dogs and letting him sleep in the bedroom with Gwen and Luwella. He'd also apologize for keeping them all up a few nights ago, but then he'd thank Arthur for not kicking him out of the bedroom forever.

And after that, he'd say he knew it was hard to be a leader but that Arthur was doing a good job and he was proud to be the dog of such a kind person.

"Cavall!"

His eyes snapped open and he bolted out of his reverie to find a figure looming over him. A figure with shaggy fur, pointed ears—one of which had a chunk torn out of it—and intense eyes the faintest shade of blue. They stared at him, into him, and he stared back, transfixed.

Then Anwen shouted, "Get away from there!" and the moment was broken.

Cavall balked, realizing he was staring into the face of a wolf, and in her mouth was Cavall's rune stone. At the sound of approaching feet, she darted across the brook and disappeared into the trees.

Anwen was at his side an instant later. "Are you all right?" she asked as he got to his feet.

He was still a little groggy from the rude awakening, but he acutely felt the missing strip of leather that he had worn every day since he'd come to Camelot. He'd grown so used to it that, for the first time, he understood what people meant when they said they felt "naked."

"We have to go after her," Anwen urged. "Come on!" She took off across the brook and into the underbrush where the wolf had disappeared.

Cavall looked back at the camp in concern. He didn't want to leave Arthur alone with Gless, but at the same time, he didn't want to abandon Anwen to chase after a dangerous animal on her own. She was tough, perhaps tougher than any other dog Cavall had ever met, but she couldn't hope to fight something that vicious alone. He gave chase, even as the people called after him to come back. He needed to help Anwen, *and* he needed to get the rune stone back.

Without it, he would never be able to lead them to the cave, and their quest would be over before it even began.

Anwen was ahead of him, but not for long. His legs carried him along the trail of mud and broken twigs she'd left in her wake. She might have the stamina for a prolonged chase, but Cavall was a sprinter. He would catch up to her soon enough.

As he barreled along, he noticed a thin mist had crept up upon them, weaving tendrils in and around the trees. It dampened the heat of the day, but made the air thick and more difficult to breathe. And it grew thicker the farther he ran. All around him, sounds became muffled, until all he heard was Anwen's muttering up ahead.

"Gonna catch that thieving wolf. Thinks she can outrace me? No way. Not with my nose. I'll track her down wherever she runs. I'll—"

Her muttering broke off abruptly. And just as abruptly, Cavall caught up to where she had stopped dead in her tracks. Too bad his legs kept carrying him forward. He crashed into her backside and slammed face-first into the ground. Leaves and grass flew up his nose, and he sneezed them out as he righted himself.

Anwen paced in circles, nose lifted and nostrils flaring. "What the . . . ?" She drew a deep sniff, waited a moment, then turned and did it again. "That's impossible."

"What?"

"The scent. It just . . . disappears." She stamped her legs. "Right here."

"Are you sure?"

She glared at him. "My nose is never wrong. It's like she just vanished."

Cavall looked around, hoping that his sight might be able to help. But the fog had become so thick he couldn't see beyond the end of his nose. The way forward was obscured, as was the way back. They were lost in a world of blankness.

"We have to find her," he said. "The rune—"

"I know, I know," Anwen grumbled. She continued to circle around, sniffing high and low. "Maybe if I could find a print or . . ." She began to wander off, picking a seemingly random direction, and disappeared into the fog.

Cavall hurried after her. He was frustrated about losing

the stone, but she seemed even more frustrated. So upset that she was willing to break one of the rules she'd pounded into his head during training: never leave the pack to tear off on your own. Perhaps she took the wolf's escape as a personal insult to her skills as a tracker?

"Anwen!" he called after her. "Slow down! We shouldn't get separated!"

When she didn't respond, he began to worry. He picked up his pace, and as he did so, he thought he might have heard a noise up ahead. Voices? Whispering to him from the mist. Whatever it was, he seemed to be drawing nearer.

Yes, those were voices. Men's voices, along with the heavy breathing of horses. That had to be Arthur and the knights. Cavall took off in a mad dash. At least if Anwen had found their way back to camp, they could get help to chase after the wolf.

Up ahead, he saw a stand of trees, just looming shadows in the fog, and that seemed to be where the voices were coming from. He must have truly gotten turned around, because this didn't look like the spot they had pitched camp earlier.

He burst through the trees, only to be met with a chorus of startled yells. A group of men—perhaps six in total—jolted from their huddled circle and snapped around to draw their swords. Half a dozen blades pointed in Cavall's direction.

Cavall took a cautious step back. This was obviously not the right camp. The men all wore strange armor and carried strange swords, much shorter than anything the knights carried. Their horses were not the ones Cavall remembered. He didn't smell Arthur among them.

A person with a funny plume on his helmet nodded toward Cavall. "A dog," he said. "You can stand down."

The people sheathed their short swords at the helmeted man's words. "Looked like a wolf in the fog," one of them said.

Cavall lowered his head to show he was no threat, that he hadn't meant to intrude on them.

The helmeted man gave him a stern look before snapping to the others, "Enough rest. We need to keep moving." He waved to the other men. "The general will be wondering where we are." He took the lead horse's reins and began leading the way through the mist. The other people followed with their own horses. All of the horses wore armor, too. It looked a little silly.

The last horse turned and looked at Cavall. "I have a feeling we've been wandering for longer than a few hours," he said, then he and his person disappeared with the others into the thick fog.

Cavall was left uncertain what to think except that he probably shouldn't follow them. They seemed as lost as him. He stood and waited until the sound of horses' hooves faded completely.

"Cavall!"

His ears perked up. That was Anwen's voice.

"Anwen!" His voice echoed back at him. "Anwen, where are you?"

He took a few steps toward where her voice had come from.

"Cavall! Why are you lagging behind? I've got something over here."

Cavall broke into a run. "I'm coming!"

"This way!"

Her voice guided him, even though there was nothing to see or smell or tell him even where he was. The fog thinned. The shapes of trees became more distinct as he followed her voice. Gradually, the forest began to take shape once more around him. Smells and sounds returned.

He came upon her tracks, where she had beaten the grass down in her mad dash. And soon he found her as well, still running madly ahead. She gave him an annoyed look over her shoulder. "Where have you been?"

Cavall didn't answer because he wasn't sure.

"She's this way," Anwen continued, eyes back on the trail ahead. "I can smell her. I can—"

She stopped short as they popped out of the bushes and right onto the shore of a babbling brook. The same babbling brook they had made camp at earlier, just farther upstream. They'd somehow made a full circle.

And no wolf, only Gless, standing on a stony outcropping, his nose pointed down toward the water. He didn't seem to notice Anwen and Cavall, because he didn't look up. "I told you not to do it," he said, though Cavall couldn't see who he might be talking to. "You fool. This is all your fault. If you hadn't been playing with magic . . ."

"You see a wolf run through here, brat?" Anwen barked.

Gless's head shot up, and Cavall had never seen his brother so startled. Or embarrassed, as if he'd been caught doing something stupid. "What are you doing here?" he demanded, quickly composing himself.

"Chasing a wolf," Anwen answered. "What are *you* doing here?"

"Well, I . . . nothing," Gless answered back haughtily, holding his head up straight. "I simply needed time away from you and those people. I don't need your idiocy rubbing off on me, now, do I?"

"You mean you left the people alone?" Cavall asked, suddenly panicked. He spun toward Anwen. "We have to get back right away."

"But the wolf—"

"The people are more important." Cavall took off at a run along the bank, back toward the camp. He heard Anwen following, and shortly after, Gless splashing across the brook to join them as well.

The sunlight setting through the trees cast long shadows, creeping as if by their own will over the forest floor. They had been gone too long, and now darkness was setting in.

The fur on the back of his neck tingled the closer he got. The rune stone was gone; he no longer had its ringing to tell him when danger was near, but something else told him to hurry, something from deep inside. His heart beat a frantic rhythm against his ribs, and he *knew* he should never have left Arthur and the others alone.

His heart slammed to a stop when a horse's frightened whinny broke like thunder through the twilight. Somewhere up ahead, metal clashed against metal. Something growled and barked. Lucan's voice screamed, "Wolf!"

The camp was under attack.

CHAPTER 9

N THE DYING LIGHT OF DAY, THE CAMP WAS IN
chaos. Packs had been torn open and their
contents scattered. Someone's bedroll had
been shredded to pieces. The horses screamed and pulled
at their bindings, trying to flee. Their panicked motions
kicked up choking dust. Arthur and the knights stood
with swords drawn, engaged in battle against an enormous . . . creature.

Lucan had called it a wolf, but it was bigger than any
wolf Cavall had seen. This animal was the size of a pony,
maybe bigger than Cavall himself, and while it had pointed

ears and a shaggy coat like a wolf, its fur was a dark, dark black. It didn't move like any animal Cavall had ever seen either, twisting and shifting so he could barely understand what he was looking at. It looked to be made not of flesh and blood, but of . . .

Shadow!

He recognized it then. This was the thing that he'd seen in the hallway that night, that had attacked Arthur. And now it was back. It snarled as it charged for Arthur once more.

Excalibur sang as it whooshed through the air and cut the giant wolf's shoulder. The animal grunted in pain, and its entire body quivered, shrank, and then began to *change*. Its back hunched, its paws became hooves, and great tusks appeared from its jaws. Right before their eyes, it had transformed from a wolf into a wild boar.

"What in the name of—?" Arthur began to ask, but the creature was on him again before he could finish, knocking him to his back on the ground. Excalibur went flying from his grasp, and he brought his hands up to protect his face.

The creature lunged with its razor-pointed tusks, but

Anwen rushed in without hesitation, barking. Cavall shook himself from his stunned staring. As he joined Anwen in falling upon the creature, Arthur scrambled for his sword.

Anwen attacked the hind legs with her powerful jaws, biting and tearing where she could. Cavall threw himself at the creature's side, trying to knock it off its hooves rather than biting at it. "Stop!" he yelled. "Why are you attacking us?"

The boar squealed, and a cold wind issued from its mouth.

"Please," he tried again, "we don't want to hurt you."

Teeth sank into his front paw and bit down. Hard.

A sharp pain ran up Cavall's leg, and he yelped. The creature shook him around like a chew rag, and Cavall could not free himself from its jaws no matter how hard he struggled. Then something barreled into the both of them with enough force to loosen its grip on him. Cavall wrenched free and took several staggering steps backward. He tripped and fell to the ground, though it took a moment to understand what had happened. Gless! His brother had driven the beast back a few paces, and the two circled each other, snarling.

"Cavall." Anwen appeared by his side. "Speak to me."

"Don't worry about me," Cavall said. He tried to stand, but his paw wouldn't work. "Please, just go help—"

"For Camelot!"

A great cry rang out, and the dogs looked up to see Lucan run headlong at the boar, sword drawn. Gless darted out of the way, and without pausing, Lucan ran the creature straight through the chest. He smiled in triumph.

Instead of falling over like a normal animal, the boar squealed again and threw Lucan off with a vicious shake of its head.

Lucan went flying and slammed into a tree with a resounding crack. It was fortunate that Lucan was wearing his armor, because the tree splintered right in half. He sank to the ground, coughing and clutching his ribs. Armor or no, he wouldn't be able to get up so quickly after that.

The boar quivered again and once more began to change. It sank to the ground. Its legs disappeared; its body became elongated; the tusks turned to vicious-looking fangs in its mouth. It had become an enormous snake, and now it was advancing on Lucan.

"No!" Bedivere raised his sword and charged. "Whatever fiendish realm you crawled out from, if you've hurt my brother—"

Before he could reach his target, the figure of a wolf—a true fur and blood wolf—burst out of the trees. The snake only had a moment to hiss angrily before the wolf snapped her jaws around its neck and gave it a good shake that sent it flying several paces back.

"Come!" she cried as she advanced on it. "Don't let it recover!" She fell on the snake again, who struck at her lightning fast with its fangs. She danced back just in time, but it was clear she would not be able to drive it off on her own.

When Cavall tried to stand, though, his wounded paw gave out under him. In frustration, he called out to the others, "Help her!" Without further direction, Anwen and Gless joined the fight.

"Keep it busy until the light is gone," the wolf commanded as they attacked the beast from three sides.

Gless charged first, snapping at it with his jaws. Then Anwen went in while it was distracted, drawing its attention to her so that the wolf could get a strike in. With all three working together, they pushed the creature to the edge of the camp. It fell back, writhing as it went. At the edge of the trees, it turned one last time, as if to announce, *I will* be back. It didn't say a word, though, simply slithered off.

A moment passed, and the last rays of light vanished from the sky.

It seemed as if a bubble had burst. Air came rushing back into the camp, and Cavall realized he was hardly breathing. In fact, everyone stopped to take in a deep breath before leaping back into action once more.

Bedivere ran to Lucan's side, while Cavall felt a hand on his shoulder and turned to see Arthur kneeling next to him. "Easy there," he said.

"What was that?" Lucan asked, and Bedivere checked him for injury.

"It was no natural animal," Arthur answered. "The way it changed . . . there must be powerful sorcery at work.

Which makes me wonder . . . what of *this* creature?"

All eyes turned to the stranger. She had pointed ears and a shaggy gray coat, with a shock of fur on her forehead. Cavall's nose recognized her. She was the wolf from the trap.

She stood watching them in return. No one moved.

"Is the human all right?" the wolf finally asked. Her eyes flickered to Bedivere helping Lucan to sit up.

"Why do you care?" Anwen snarled.

"She risked her life to help us," Cavall pointed out. Then to her, "Why *did* you help us?"

"I wanted to help the human who saved my life." She flattened her ears against her head. "May I see if he's all right?"

"You have some nerve," Anwen huffed, "stealing Cavall's rune stone and then—"

"Anwen, I don't think she's the thief," Cavall interrupted.

"What do you mean? Of course she is. She's the one we've been chasing all afternoon. I can smell it."

She did smell a little bit . . . a lot like the scent they'd followed into the forest. "But why would she come back to help us in that case?"

"I don't know. Maybe it's a trick. Hey! Where are you going?"

The wolf had apparently grown tired of their bickering and headed toward Lucan of her own accord.

"Don't you dare—"

"Let her go, Anwen," Cavall said. "If she wanted to hurt Lucan, she wouldn't have tried to save him."

"We shouldn't be letting this happen. Wolves are dangerous."

"I think she just wants to thank him for saving her life."

Anwen huffed but didn't protest further.

Bedivere saw the wolf first and tried to wave her away, the way people did to Cavall when they didn't want to share their food with him. "Gah!" he hollered. "Go on! Get!"

But the wolf just kept approaching. Lucan, still clutching his side and breathing heavily, shushed Bedivere. "She won't hurt me."

"You don't know that."

"I do." Lucan held out his other hand.

The wolf sniffed and came closer. Eventually, she nudged her nose under his hand. Lucan smiled and gave her a gentle pat. She laid her ears flat against her head and came closer still.

Lucan continued to pet her gently. "Thank you," he whispered.

CHAPTER 10

"So, you found yourself a new friend," Bedivere said. "I don't suppose we could find you new ribs, too."

Lucan winced as he poked at his side. The wolf, sitting beside him, pricked up her ears at his distress. "They're just bruised," Lucan insisted. "You should see to Arthur."

"I'm not hurt," Arthur answered. "Though I fear Cavall is." He touched Cavall's front paw where the creature had bitten him. Even though he was gentle, Cavall yelped. "I'm sorry," Arthur said quickly.

Cavall licked his face to show he didn't blame him.

"Bedivere's bandaging up Lucan. Let's see if we can't do the same for you." Arthur ripped a strip of cloth from the torn bedroll and wrapped it around Cavall's paw. His eyebrows creased as he tried to be both gentle and tight with the bindings. Eventually, he had wrapped it several times, and Cavall had to admit that it felt better once it was covered. Arthur finished by patting Cavall's flank. "Do you think you can stand, boy?"

Cavall got to his feet. It hurt to put weight on the injured paw, but he took a few limping steps.

Bedivere shook his head. "This will slow us down."

"Then it will slow us down," Arthur said. He sighed and rubbed at the back of his neck. Cavall knew it must be frustrating for him, knowing every minute they wasted was a minute Mordred could not spare. Still, he was glad his person was willing to protect his friends instead of leaving them behind.

Arthur stood and surveyed the mess of the camp. Since the first priority had been tending the wounded members of their party, no one had really done a damage check.

While everyone checked themselves and each other for

wounds, Gless wandered off and sat on the bank of the river, his usual aloof demeanor back. Cavall considered going over to thank him for his help during the attack, but his brother looked like he wanted to be alone.

Darkness had fully set, and with it came the strange silence that announced the fay awakening. Arthur gave the go-ahead to start a fire. "I doubt we'll be able to keep our presence here secret, fire or not," he said as he took off his armor.

"We could all do for a bit of warmth," Bedivere agreed.

He gathered wood while Arthur collected the scattered packs. Most of the rations remained intact. The thing that had attacked them had not wanted their food. The wolf was interested, though. Cavall noticed her inching closer to the dried meat, nostrils sniffing. Anwen noticed this, too. She bared her teeth and snapped, "Leave that alone!"

The wolf fled for the safety of the trees and stood there watching them.

"Anwen, she helped us," Cavall reminded her.

"Well, then she's helped us. Now she can go on her way."

As they argued, the wolf crept closer again. "The garmr

will return," she said. "A garmr always returns."

"A what?" Anwen asked.

"The creature that's been following you since before you even entered the forest," the wolf explained. "A garmr is a shadow creature, a guardian of the underworld. Wherever they go, bad things follow. It will keep coming back until it has what it wants."

"What does it want?" Cavall remembered how the creature had attacked them in the royal bedroom a few nights ago and was pretty sure he already knew the answer.

His eyes met the wolf's. "It wants one of you dead."

A chill ran down Cavall's spine, all the way to the tip of his tail.

"Or maybe you're just yanking our tails," Anwen said, giving the wolf a skeptical eye. "Maybe you're just telling us this story so you can steal more from us, hmm?"

If Cavall had the rune stone, it would tell him whether he could trust this wolf or not. But since he didn't, and it couldn't, he would have to go with his gut feeling. "I don't think she's the thief," he said, limping to put himself between Anwen and the stranger.

"You said that earlier," Anwen said, "but my nose is never wrong."

"What is it you think I stole?" the wolf asked, cocking her head.

"My collar," Cavall explained. "It had a magic rune stone on it that was leading us . . . somewhere." He wasn't sure if he should mention the cave or not. "A wolf stole it while I was sleeping." He nodded toward the brook. "But I don't think it was you. The wolf I saw had blue eyes, and you . . . don't." He wasn't sure what color her eyes were, but they definitely weren't the pale blue ones he had seen looking down at him when he'd woken with a start.

"You saw another wolf around here?" The wolf twitched her ears thoughtfully. Then, with a disappointed sigh, she said, "It must have been my sister, Gudrun. She's always stealing things."

"A likely story," Anwen said with a roll of her eyes.

"I keep telling her that stealing things won't bring them back."

"Them? Who's 'them'?" Cavall asked.

The wolf shook her head. "No one. It's something our

mother used to tell us when we were pups." She raised her head. "I'm sorry she's made trouble for you."

"More than trouble," Anwen groused.

"The rune stone she stole was a gift from a friend," Cavall explained. "It's really very important we get it back." Not to mention how helpless he felt without it.

The wolf swished her tail thoughtfully. "I can take you to my sister. If we explain the situation to her, I'm sure she'll agree to return it to you. Only..." Her eyes flicked to the people, who were still putting the camp back together. "She doesn't like humans very much...at all."

Bedivere passed by them, his arms laden with sticks. He eyed them all warily, especially the wolf, then tilted his head. "Come, dogs."

"In any case," Anwen said, shaking out her ears, "we won't be traveling any more tonight." She followed Bedivere back to camp.

Cavall hated to admit it, but she was right. It would be too dangerous to keep going. He got painfully to his feet. "You're welcome to join us for the rest of night if you'd like," he said to the wolf.

She looked from him to the people and back. Her ears twitched. "Thank you." She dipped her head. "I am Astrus, by the way."

"I'm Cavall."

As they approached camp, they found Bedivere kneeling over a pile of sticks, furiously rubbing two together. "Watch this," he announced. "I'll show you how a real fire starter does it." Cavall watched, fascinated, as the twigs began to smoke, and a moment later, a tiny tendril of fire burst to life. Bedivere grinned in triumph.

Then he *tsk*ed as he caught sight of Astrus standing next to Cavall.

"What is that beast still doing here? Shoo, shoo!"

"Leave her be, Bedivere," Lucan called. He had taken off his armor and was now clutching his side as he sat next to Arthur. "A meal is the least we can do for her after she helped us fend off that monster."

"That monster, yes," Arthur murmured. The light from the slowly growing fire danced in his eyes, and his thoughts seemed to be far away at the moment. "I wonder what that creature was. It seemed . . . most unnatural." Cavall felt him shudder slightly. Perhaps he was remembering that night in the castle as well.

Astrus approached Lucan with her tail down, and Lucan reached out for her again and scratched her ears. "This is the strangest wolf I've ever met." He laughed.

"Met many wolves, have you?" Bedivere laughed back.

The knight tended the flame until it grew into a strong fire. The warmth was very nice. Even Gless abandoned his lonely position on the riverbank to warm himself by the fire, though he stopped short of sitting next to anyone. Which was too bad because Cavall wanted to thank him for his help during the attack. And ask about the strange scene he and Anwen had stumbled upon earlier.

"At least the rations are still intact," Arthur announced, reaching into his pack. He pulled out some dried meat, broke it in two, and handed the larger chunk to Cavall. "Here, boy, you deserve this."

Cavall took it gratefully with a wag of his tail.

"They . . . feed you?"

Cavall looked up at Astrus's question and found her staring wide-eyed at his food.

"The humans feed you?" she asked again. "Just like that?"

Her gaze shifted over to Bedivere, who gave Anwen a piece of meat from his own pack but froze when he caught the wolf staring. "Should I . . . ?"

"Oh, give her something to eat," Lucan called as he handed a bit to Gless.

Bedivere looked uncertain, and instead of offering Astrus food from his hand, he tossed the hunk of meat. The wolf ran after it and tore at it with her teeth. Bedivere grimaced. "Glad that wasn't my hand."

Astrus swallowed her food and licked her lips. "I will lead you to my sister," she said, "but you must promise not to hurt her."

"We don't want to hurt her," Cavall said. "We just want to get the rune stone back. I trust you to lead us there."

"If Cavall trusts you, I trust you." Anwen sighed, as if in defeat. "Never thought I'd see the day when I'd team up with a wolf, but there it is."

Everyone sat in silence. Beyond the circle of light cast by the fire, a chorus of sounds faded in and out—the hooting of an owl, the chittering of animals in the trees, the hushed whisper of voices.

"I'll take first watch tonight," Arthur offered.

Neither Lucan nor Bedivere argued. They both looked exhausted. Anwen burrowed in with Bedivere, and Gless found shelter under a rock outcropping. Astrus curled up within a long arm's reach of Lucan, close enough and yet far enough for them both to be comfortable.

Arthur sat tending the fire, allowing it to burn low. Cavall sat at his side and soaked up the last heat of the dying embers.

"I don't know what I did to deserve such loyal friends," Arthur said, rubbing Cavall's ears, "but I'm sure I would be lost without them. You know . . ." He stared deep into the coals of the fire, never taking his hands from Cavall's ears, "I have not had a bad dream since I saw you standing against that awful creature from my nightmares. I think you must be my dream protector." He sighed heavily. "The physician believes Mordred is lost somewhere in the Dreaming right now, so I was hoping . . . might you look after him as you have done for me?"

Cavall licked the hand that had been scratching him. He wasn't sure Arthur would understand, but Arthur smiled anyway.

"Aye, you're a good pup. I'm glad I didn't listen to Mordred and took you for my hound. Mordred is my son, and I will always love him, but . . ." He looked around, as if he suspected someone was listening in on them. "He is not a good judge of character."

Cavall had never heard his person talk this way about Mordred. "You can tell me anything," he said. But of course Arthur couldn't understand him, so he licked his person's face to show him. He'd tell him again once he got Gelert's Wish.

But how was he going to find the cave where Gelert's Wish was hidden—or, at least, where he *hoped* Gelert's Wish was hidden—if he didn't have his rune stone? He could only hope that Astrus could convince her sister to return it. He felt exposed and vulnerable without its vibrations warning him of danger.

As the night wore on, he jumped at every noise from the forest, every rustle of leaves and snapping of twigs. Astrus had said the shadow creature would return, but without the aid of his rune stone, how was he to know when?

Somehow, he didn't think he would be sleeping much tonight.

 AVALL WOKE UP TO SOMEONE NUDGING HIM roughly in the side. It took half a moment to remember where they were—deep in the fay woods with a dangerous animal on the prowl. He bolted out of sleep and looked around for danger, but found only Gless glaring at him. His brother stood with his shoulders hunched, head down and swinging from side to side as if on the lookout for something. It was still dark, though a faint line of blue had appeared in the sky.

"Cavall," he hissed, "we need to get going."

"But it's still night. The fay—"

"We need to get going now," Gless said.

Cavall looked around the camp. Arthur was still asleep by his side. Bedivere stood watch with Anwen by a tree. Lucan lay stretched out where he had fallen asleep; Bedivere had apparently not woken him for his shift. By his side, Astrus lifted her head and watched them.

"Can't we wait until dawn?" Cavall asked. "It's not much longer now, and it will be safer to travel then."

"No, he's right," Astrus said, standing. "The garmr is a creature of shadow. It's strongest when the shadows are long, just as the sun rises and before it sets."

"How do you know that?" Gless demanded.

"How do *you*?" she asked back.

Gless's nostrils flared. He did not like being challenged. "Let's get the people up," he said, stalking away without answering her question. "We can't afford to be sitting around when the shadows grow long."

Cavall wondered how Gless knew to be up before dawn to evade the garmr but decided not to question him. If Astrus was right, they couldn't waste time arguing.

His wounded paw was stiff as he stood and nudged

Arthur awake. Arthur groaned and opened his eyes. "Is it morning already?"

"What?" Bedivere asked, turning from his lookout position by the tree. "No."

"The dogs . . ." Arthur sat up and stretched his arms over his head. "Well, it's close enough, and I'm awake now. What do you say, Lucan?"

Lucan coughed.

"Lucan? Are you all right?" Bedivere came over to his brother's side.

"It's . . . nothing," Lucan insisted, but winced when Bedivere pressed fingers against the spot where he'd been tossed against the tree yesterday.

Bedivere frowned. "You may have broken a rib or two," he said with a cluck of his tongue.

"Perhaps . . . ," Lucan gasped, "you should go on without me."

"And leave you for that monster to finish off?" Arthur shook his head. "Come on, get to your feet. We're close to the Holy Grail; I just know it."

Lucan sighed. "Very well, but give me a minute."

He was in a bad way if he couldn't even stand on his own. If they could just get him to the Holy Grail, with its healing power . . .

"We need to help him," Cavall said. He hadn't been too concerned with finding the Grail when they'd set out, but now that Lucan needed it, he felt an urgency that hadn't been there before. "We need to get him up."

Astrus nodded.

Lucan looked quizzically from dog to wolf as they drew near, like a cornered animal unsure if it was about to be attacked or not. He let out a surprised *oomph* as Astrus put her nose under his arm and nudged him from the left. Cavall did the same on the right, and Anwen nipped at his feet, the way she sometimes did to dogs who lagged behind during hunting lessons.

"You're wasting your time," Gless said, watching but not helping. "The weak and wounded should be left behind."

"We're *not* leaving him," Astrus said.

Gless heaved a weary sigh. "Nobody ever listens to me." He shook his head and trotted toward them. "All right, if it makes us move faster, let's get him on his feet." He took one of Lucan's sleeves in his teeth. Astrus caught on and took the other sleeve, and together they tugged. Cavall used his height to push the man from behind. Eventually, Lucan was forced to either stand up or be pulled over.

Arthur and Bedivere stood watching in amazement. "Did you suddenly acquire the power to charm beasts, brother?" Bedivere asked.

Lucan laughed, then clutched his side like it hurt. "I'm not doing anything, I promise. I have no idea what's gotten into these animals."

"They want you to finish the quest," Arthur said, beaming. "It's a sign that we're not far. Here, Bedivere, let's help him up on his horse."

Lucan groaned as they hoisted him up onto his saddle. "I . . . hope you're right . . . Arthur," he panted, still holding his ribs. "I don't know . . . how long I can . . . ride like this."

Astrus yipped and bounded forward. Arthur and Bedivere looked to each other in confusion. "I think she wants us to follow her," Bedivere said.

Cavall took a few limping paces after her, then turned and looked over his shoulder at the people.

"I think Cavall wants us to follow her as well," Arthur said.

"Are you sure that's wise?" Bedivere asked, a troubled look on his face.

"Merlin said Cavall would lead the way," Arthur said, climbing onto his horse. "I trust Merlin, and, more important, I trust Cavall."

Cavall's heart pounded at that. Every day since he'd first come to Camelot, he'd wanted nothing more than for Arthur to trust him. But Arthur trusted him to lead them to the Holy Grail—what would he say if he knew Cavall was only interested in finding Gelert's Wish? Or had been before Lucan became injured. And what would Arthur say if he knew it wasn't Cavall, but the stone that had been leading them all this time? And now the stone was gone. He needed to get it back as soon as possible. Then he would deal with the matter of Gelert's Wish and the Holy Grail, when he was able to lead them once again.

They began at a steady pace, though Gless kept urging them to go faster. Luckily for Cavall's wounded paw, Astrus took the lead and maintained a pace slow enough that he could keep up with her. He didn't limp so badly if he walked more heavily on his good paw, but it was still nice to have Anwen keeping in step with him and nudging him on whenever he stumbled. All of them kept alert for any sign of the garmr.

The sun came up over the trees, and Cavall watched nervously as the shadows grew long. The trees in this part of the forest were twisted things, their thick trunks bent with age and gnarled with knotholes. Their crooked branches, draped with hairy hanging moss, cast shadows that played tricks on his eyes. Here he thought he saw a snake; over there was an enormous boar.

He remained on edge, turning at every rustle in the leaves, at every chirping of the birds in the trees or animals on the ground. He thought he heard a low growl from a cluster of bushes, but no one else seemed to hear it.

The sun came up and the shadow creature did not make a reappearance.

As the shadows grew smaller the higher the sun rose, the party's nerves faded. Soon, Anwen was casting suspicious glances toward Astrus instead of the forest.

"Why did your sister steal the rune stone?" she asked at last.

Astrus kept her gaze locked ahead. She had a strange way of walking, hunched over, as if on the prowl. "She believes it will impress the Ulfsfadir and bring him back."

"Ulfsfadir?" Cavall tried the funny word for himself.

He must not have done too well, because Astrus pulled a face. "Wolf Father," she clarified. "A powerful fay, the father of the First Guardian."

They all had to duck, except for Anwen, as they passed under a low-hanging branch. The moss swept over Cavall's back, wet and slimy. The people paused before steering their horses completely around the tree to join them on the other side. Cavall checked to make sure they were still behind and then called up to Astrus, "Remember that the people can't follow us as easily."

"Right, sorry." Astrus gave him a sheepish look. "I'll try to remember."

"Wolf Father," Anwen said, apparently still mulling over Astrus's words. "Why does that sound familiar?"

"I've heard that before, too." Cavall thought for a

moment. It had been just a short time ago. "Drudwyn!" he exclaimed as the memory surged back. "Drudwyn had a story about an ancient fay who liked to steal things. He said Wolf Father was one of his many names."

"Ah, that makes sense," Anwen said. She scrabbled over a mossy rock, short legs working overtime to keep her from slipping. "Say, wolf . . . if you know about this Wolf Father, you must know about the cave where he supposedly hid all his treasures."

Astrus froze midstep over a raised tree root, ears flattened against her head. "N-no."

Anwen snorted dramatically and trotted to catch up with her. The small dog looked up at the considerably larger wolf, nose to nose, eyes issuing a hard challenge. "I can smell a lie as well as I can smell a deer, you know."

Astrus finished hopping over the root and kept walking. "It . . . it's supposed to be a secret."

Anwen slipped under the root, obviously intent on not letting the matter slip. "And the Holy Grail? Is that supposed to be a secret, too?"

Astrus's eyes shifted left to right.

Cavall loped up to her other side and pressed himself in. "You can't tell us anything about the cave?" he prodded. If she could confirm that Gelert's Wish was actually there . . .

"W-well . . . ," Astrus began.

"Enough!" Gless broke from his place in their line and threw himself in front of Astrus, forcing her to stop.

"Gless," Cavall cried. "What are you—?"

"Tell us what you know about the cave and the Holy Grail," Gless barked.

Arthur's horse whinnied with indignation at the sudden holdup.

"What's this?" Arthur demanded, pulling on the horse's reins. "What's gotten into you dogs?"

"Gless has started a fight," Bedivere said.

Lucan coughed.

They didn't have time for this. "Gless, stop!" Cavall head-butted his brother in the shoulder. "You said you wouldn't—"

"Leave her alone, dog!" A shape burst out of the trees and slammed into Gless, knocking him back. At first,

Cavall thought it was the shadow monster, come to finish what it had started. But as he jumped into action, he realized it was another wolf, and that she had placed herself between Gless and Astrus, teeth bared and a low growl issuing from deep in her throat.

Her eyes met his. They were the same blue he had seen looking down at him yesterday. When he'd woken up to find his rune stone missing.

"Let me guess," Anwen growled. "That's the sister we've been looking for."

CHAPTER 12

"GUDRUN, STOP," ASTRUS PLEADED.

"They were attacking you," the other wolf snarled, not backing down. Every hackle on her back was raised as she glared at the dogs, and especially Gless.

"No, they weren't. Just let me explain."

Gless and the new wolf—Gudrun—ignored her, circling each other with murderous looks mirrored in their eyes. Cavall glanced at the people and was relieved to find them keeping their distance. Though Bedivere had a hand firmly on the hilt of his sword.

"So," Gless sneered, pacing to match Gudrun's every move, "you're the one who stole my brother's rune stone."

"If you've hurt my sister in any way," Gudrun said back, "I'll tear you into little pieces."

The air was as tense as a plucked string. Someone needed to calm the situation down right away. Apparently Astrus had the same thought, because just as Cavall stepped in front of Gless, Astrus stepped in front of her sister. Gless tried to look around Cavall, but Cavall's larger frame kept him from doing so.

"What are you doing, Cavall?" Gless snarled.

"Move aside, Astrus," Gudrun said.

"What's going on up there?" Lucan asked. He probably couldn't see much from his horse at the back of the line.

"It's another wolf," Bedivere said. "But this one doesn't appear too friendly." He looked to Arthur. "What do you think, Your Majesty? Should I . . . ?"

Arthur drew his lips into a tight line. "Well . . ."

Cavall's heart seized. The last thing they needed was for a fight to break out. Then they might never get the rune stone back and never find the cave, let alone Gelert's

Wish *or* the Holy Grail.

He swung his head toward where the people hung back several paces and searched for his person's eyes. "You said you trusted me earlier," Cavall said, even though Arthur wouldn't understand, "so please trust me. Don't attack the wolves."

A moment passed between them, where everything around them seemed to fade—the wolves, the forest, even their divided quest for the Holy Grail and Gelert's Wish. It felt as if Arthur was searching as intently for understanding between them as Cavall was.

Finally, Arthur's face softened and he rubbed at the back of his neck. "Don't draw your sword, Bedivere."

Bedivere let the hand on his sword hilt fall away without question, though he looked unconvinced. Cavall let out a relieved breath.

"Cavall, what are you doing?" Gless growled. "She stole your rune stone. We can take it back from her by force if she won't give it back on her own."

"No," Cavall said, "not like that."

He needed to speak with Gudrun, but he didn't dare turn his back on Gless, lest he try to start a fight again.

Anwen sniffed indignantly. "Now, listen up, brat." She marched up to Gless, body quivering with anger. "You promised to follow my orders on this quest, so here's an order for you. Back down."

Gless glowered at her.

She glowered right back, even more fiercely. "Right now."

Grumbling, Gless backed away and plopped his hindquarters in the dirt. His angry gaze never left the wolf sisters.

Cavall nodded gratefully to Anwen, then turned to face the wolves. "Gudrun," he announced, "my name is Cavall. I don't want to hurt you. I think you have something that belongs to me."

Gudrun snorted. "If I found it, it belongs to me now."

"*Gudrun*," Astrus scolded. "If you stole their stone, you should return it to them."

Gudrun flattened her ears against her head. Even though her hackles hadn't gone all the way down, she no longer seemed ready to lunge at any moment. "I don't have your stupid stone."

"Please," Cavall said, stepping forward. Gudrun backed away. "We need it back."

"Our companion is dying," Gless said, much to everyone's surprise. "Back in Camelot. And every moment we waste arguing with you is a moment he grows closer to death. We need that rune stone to save him, and we're running out of time."

Cavall lifted his head in surprise. Gless hadn't said anything about coming on this quest for *Mordred's* sake.

"Why should I care about your friend?" Gudrun said. "No human or dog has ever cared about us."

Astrus's ear twitched as she nodded toward Arthur and the others. "These humans and dogs saved my life. They cut me free from a trap."

"A trap *they* laid," Gudrun shot back.

"You need to return what you stole from them, Gudrun." Astrus puffed out her chest, bringing herself to her full height. "I've told you a thousand times, stealing things won't bring the Ulfsfadir back, it won't bring the First Guardian back, and it certainly won't bring Mother back."

Gudrun reeled as if she'd been struck.

But Astrus continued. "If you won't return it to them, then *I'll* lead them to your hiding place."

Gudrun surged forward. "You can't!"

"I can."

"Mother told us not to reveal the cave to anyone." She eyed the rest of them as if they might attack her at any moment. "Especially not to human lovers like you."

Cavall blinked. He'd never been called a "human lover" before.

"So," Anwen began with a wry chuckle, causing everyone to look at her. Cavall didn't see anything funny about the situation. "Another one of Drudwyn's stories is true. There *is* a cave full of stolen treasures, and there *is* a guardian to this cave. But it's not a giant wolf. It's you two, isn't it?"

Gudrun's blue eyes widened in surprise, before they quickly narrowed again, directing a withering look at her sister. "You should have kept your maw shut."

"But, Gudrun, think about it," Astrus said. "The prophecy says someone worthy will be allowed into the Crystal Cave." She looked over Cavall's shoulder to where the people still waited for a decision to be made. "Maybe they're the ones."

"Why? Because one human set you free instead of killing you? You think that makes them worthy?" Gudrun shook her head in disgust. She turned with a flick of her shaggy tail. "What would the Ulfsfadir say if he returned to find his cave plundered, hmm?"

Astrus wrinkled her snout. "If the Ulfsfadir wants his treasures protected so badly," she snapped, "then he can come and protect them himself." She came to stand between Cavall and Anwen, placing herself squarely on their side. "Perhaps *that* will bring him back."

Gudrun stared at her for a long moment. "You're making a mistake, trusting them. They'll turn on you the minute you've given them what they want."

"Or maybe," Astrus replied, standing strong, "they deserve the chance to prove themselves worthy."

Gudrun snarled. "Fine. Have it your way. But the day I help a human or a dog is the day the underworld's gates are flung wide-open. If I see them anywhere near the cave, I'll perform my duty as guardian. One of us has to." With that, she darted off into the woods and disappeared from view.

CHAPTER 13

THE SUN WAS HIGH AND THE DAY WAS HOT. THE people occasionally wiped the sweat from their faces and necks, while the dogs panted in the afternoon heat. The shade from the trees was comforting, though the shadows remained a constant reminder of the garmr's return.

"I'm sorry we caused you and your sister to fight," Cavall said as they walked along, head low and tongue lolling from his mouth.

Astrus took a deep breath. She didn't seem at all bothered by the sweltering heat, despite her thick fur. "It's not your fault." She looked over her shoulder to Gless, who plodded along with a sour look on his face. "Brothers and sisters are difficult to get along with sometimes, aren't they?"

Cavall couldn't disagree with that.

"Do you think she'll try to keep us from getting to the cave?"

Astrus thought for a moment. "She might," she admitted at last. "If she does, can you keep your promise not to hurt her?" She hung her head, as if in shame. "Even if we fight, that doesn't mean I want her to get hurt."

Cavall looked to Gless, who caught him staring and looked back.

"If it's at all possible," he answered Astrus, "we won't hurt her."

They walked along in silence for a while, having to break for water often, or whenever Lucan's coughing became too intense. Arthur and Bedivere would help him from his horse and pat him on the back until the fit passed. Then Arthur would make him drink from the water skin before they both helped him back up. Traveling this way was slow going.

They crested a small hill, and for a brief moment, everyone paused.

Spread out before them lay a field of blue. Tiny flowers, Cavall realized as they drew closer, shaped like little bells, three and four to a stalk. They covered the entire forest floor, bobbing happily in the slight breeze. Their fragrance filled the air.

Bedivere bent to pick one and drew a deep breath. "Bluebells," he announced. "Fairy flowers. We're in a fay clearing, to be sure."

"Then tread lightly," Arthur said. "We are guests here and must remain respectful."

Astrus led the way through the flowers, a jaunty step to her gait. Her paws didn't bend a single petal, almost as if they moved to make way for her. Cavall and the others followed behind.

"The entrance isn't very far now," Astrus said. "Sometimes it's hard to find." Then, almost to herself, "I hope I can find it again."

Cavall hoped she could, too.

Up ahead, an enormous rock jutted crookedly out of the ground, taller than it was wide, with images engraved on its surface. Cavall recognized it. He'd seen a rock just like this on the day he'd met Arthur, also in the middle of the woods, though this one was smaller and more weatherworn. The images were difficult to make out, partly because they were so old and partly because the rock was covered in moss and ivy where the forest was slowly reclaiming it. As he looked closer, the engravings seemed to glow a faint blue, which made the picture stand out.

It was a wolf. He recognized the shape by now. Its teeth were bared in a snarl, and its nose pointed toward the crescent moon over its head. And at its feet . . . were those bushes? With their twisted branches, they were obviously meant to be plants of some sort, but . . .

Cavall blinked. Those weren't supposed to be *trees*, were they? They were so much tinier than the wolf. How big was the wolf supposed to *be*?

"Oh," Astrus said. "That's Fenrir, the First Guardian. Mother told us he was a giant and a fay himself, and wherever he walked, he left big holes with his paws that turned into lakes."

Cavall looked up, as if a giant wolf might walk right

over them at any moment. But he only saw the blue sky overhead.

"He's been gone for almost as long as the Wolf Father," Astrus explained. "He was his son, after all. When the Wolf Father was called away, he left Fenrir to guard the Crystal Cave, and that's how our line became the guardians. The prophecy of the cave says that in the event he never returns, a worthy soul will be allowed to take its treasures."

"Is that so?" Anwen scrunched up her face. "And just who gave you this prophecy?"

"The cave did," Astrus answered.

"How can a cave *give* you a prophecy?" Anwen asked, putting into words what Cavall was thinking.

"Well, it . . ." Astrus furrowed her brow as she thought. "It's a . . . there's this voice and . . ." She sighed in frustration. "You'll have to see for yourself. It's possible the cave won't like you very much at all, but I don't think that's likely."

Now Cavall was more confused than ever. She spoke of the cave as if it were alive and had a mind of its own.

But caves were just big holes in the ground, weren't they? He suddenly had a terrifying image of a great, gaping mouth waiting to swallow them all up for daring to enter. As frightening as that was, he knew they'd come too far to turn back now. If the cave did have a mind of its own, maybe it could be reasoned with. Surely when it saw how badly Lucan was hurt, it would agree to let them in to get the Holy Grail. And then he could search for Gelert's Wish, once Lucan was out of danger.

Cavall was beginning to think of this cave as a person, perhaps a slightly grumpy one he would have to win over.

The sky began to darken, and there was still no sign of a cave.

"That tree!" Anwen cried suddenly. Her nostrils flared. "I've smelled that tree before. You've been taking us around in circles."

"I'm sure that's not true," Cavall said. "The forest just looks the same, that's all."

But a few moments later, they came upon the standing stone again. There was no denying, they were doubling back to where they began.

"I . . . I'm sorry," Astrus said. "I *know* the entrance to the cave is around here somewhere, I just . . ." Her ears flicked back and forth.

"Well, if you could hurry up," Anwen grumped. "It's getting dark, and if we don't find your cave soon, not only will we have a gam . . . a garm . . . a *whatever* to contend with, but all the fay in the forest as well."

"It's here," Astrus repeated.

"You better not be leading us on a wild-hare chase," Gless muttered darkly.

They continued walking. The shadows passed over them like birds of prey, growing longer and longer as the sun set. Cavall imagined the garmr could be hiding in any one of them.

Lucan coughed.

A twig snapped behind them.

Cavall whirled around, accidentally putting too much weight on his injured paw as he did so. He yelped at the fresh pain.

"Just keep moving," Astrus whispered by his side. "We're almost—"

Suddenly, her head shot up, eyes locked straight ahead.

Cavall followed her gaze toward the thick mist rolling in. It radiated an ethereal light in the glow of the setting sun.

"That's it," she said. "Follow close behind me and—"

Something in the corner of his eyes moved. Cavall whipped his head around, just in time to see a shape break free from the shadows off to their left. It moved with incredible speed, rising up and taking form. A thick body on four long, thin legs, with many-pronged antlers jutting from its head—it had become a stag made of pure darkness.

The garmr had returned.

For a moment, nobody moved. Nobody breathed.

Then the garmr bellowed and charged for the horses. Gless was faster. The horses screamed, and Gless darted into the shadow's oncoming path. He stood tall, challenging. He didn't flinch; neither did the creature. It lowered its antlers, aiming their sharp points right at Gless's throat.

Cavall reacted. The earth moved under his paws seemingly of its own will. The distance between him, his brother, and the shadow creature shrank. And in the blink of an eye, Cavall threw himself right at the beast.

He collided with it, and together they tumbled head over tail. The world spun around and around as Cavall tried to get back to his paws. He seemed to have thrown the garmr, because it staggered as well.

Arthur's horse reared back and nearly bucked him off, but Arthur held tight and got the animal under control. "It's the beast again," he cried, drawing Excalibur from the sheath at his side. "Bedivere, ride with Lucan to safety. I'll fend it off."

"Your Majesty," Bedivere protested, but Arthur had already charged at the garmr. Excalibur swished through the air and struck the creature in its neck. Such a blow should have severed its head, but instead, the shadow retreated, melting into an indefinite shape before rearing up once more and re-forming.

Everyone stood frozen, preparing for what it would turn into next.

"This way!" Astrus gave a sharp howl that had even Arthur turning to look for the sound. "The entrance is up here." She jerked her head toward the mist. "Follow me."

"She knows where to go," Lucan said.

"Or perhaps she's saving her own hide," Bedivere announced.

"It seems the same to me."

The monster had become an enormous eagle. Its shriek echoed through the forest as it took to the sky, flapping wings as long as a person's arm span. It circled around, then swooped down, razor-pointed talons aimed straight for Arthur, who raised his sword to meet the creature.

"No!" Cavall struggled to his feet. "You can't win against it."

Even if he could somehow get a strike in, the monster would just re-form itself and come back for another attack. They couldn't keep battling a creature they didn't even know how to fight. Astrus had the right idea.

Cavall put all of his strength into his bark. He felt it build in his chest, up into his throat, and then released it into a massive noise that shook every flower in the forest like a thousand little warning bells.

Arthur swung around, missing the shadow monster's talons by the mere breadth of a hair. "Cavall, what—?"

Cavall barked again, less forcefully. Ran a few paces

toward where Astrus had disappeared. Stopped and looked back.

"He wants us to follow the wolf," Lucan said.

Arthur gritted his teeth and shot a furtive glance toward the monster, circling back around for another attack. "I suppose it's the best chance we have. Lucan! Bedivere! With me!" He brought his horse around and whistled sharply for the dogs.

Bedivere grabbed Lucan's horse by the reins and spurred them both onward.

They fled into the mist. The trees disappeared around them. So did the sun and shadows. There was only Astrus's howl ahead and the garmr's angry cries from behind.

Cavall tried not to think of the pain in his paw or what would happen if he tripped. Instead, he focused on Arthur's horse just ahead of him and the way Arthur kept glancing over his shoulder to make sure Cavall was still there. He thought about how Lucan must be in much more pain than him and was still keeping up with the others. He thought of Gelert's Wish and the Holy Grail and what they would do with these treasures once they had them.

His heart beat wildly in his throat.

"I see something!" someone shouted. Cavall couldn't hear who over the pounding in his ears. But he could see. Up ahead, the mists had thinned. The forest began to re-form around them, as well as something new. The yawning maw of a cave, partially obscured by thick forest growth. That was it, Cavall was sure.

Astrus disappeared through the curtain of vines. Lucan and Bedivere rode in after her, and then Anwen and Gless.

"Hurry!" Arthur called to Cavall. "We can make it."

We. He wasn't going to leave Cavall behind, even when he could urge his own horse on faster.

Cavall couldn't see what was on the other side, but he knew that the beast would be gaining on them soon. Together, he and Arthur plunged through the curtain of mossy vines and disappeared with the others.

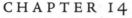

CHAPTER 14

 AVALL BLINKED AGAINST THE BLINDING LIGHT. He hadn't expected to find such brightness on the other side, like the shining of the midday sun. Hundreds of glittering rocks covered the cave's walls, bathing everything in a pale blue light.

Everyone stood gawking for a moment. Then Lucan began coughing again, and Arthur and Bedivere scrambled from their horses to help him. Cavall looked behind, waiting for the shadow creature to come bursting through and attack them.

"It won't follow us in here," Astrus said. "The light

here is too bright for it."

Lucan had stopped coughing, but the scent of blood clung to him. "He can't ride anymore, Arthur," Bedivere said, helping his brother down to the ground.

"With luck we won't *have* to ride anymore," Arthur answered. He reached for his water skin and handed it to Lucan, who drank thirstily from it. "This will be a good place to defend ourselves if that creature attacks again. We'll make camp here." He touched a gloved hand against one of the shining rocks. "These crystals are incredible. This *must* be the cave Merlin spoke of. If the Holy Grail is to be found, it must certainly be here."

"I've never seen anything like it," Bedivere agreed. "The wolf truly knew where she was leading us."

Lucan looked like he was about to say something when he keeled forward onto his hands and knees and began coughing even harder than before. Specks of blood fell from his lips, and he looked very pale as Bedivere got him back into a sitting position. "I'm . . . fine," he murmured, looking very *not* fine.

"We need to hurry if Lucan is to stand a chance," Cavall

said. "Can you take us to the Grail?"

The white mark on Astrus's forehead furrowed as she gave him an apologetic look. "I'm afraid it's . . . not that easy."

"Not that easy?!" Anwen and Gless cried at the same time, in the same disbelieving tone.

Astrus glanced down the mouth of the cave, covered with thousands of iridescent crystals and stretching so far back that Cavall couldn't see the end of it. "The inner chamber, where all the treasures are kept, is . . . blocked. Only those who prove themselves worthy can get through."

"Well, what do we need to do to prove ourselves worthy?" Cavall asked.

"The Wolf Father set up three tasks that must be solved before anyone can set paw in the inner cavern."

Gless eyed her skeptically. "What sort of tasks?"

"It doesn't matter," Cavall blurted. All eyes turned to him as he got to his feet. Suppressing a grimace at the pain in his paw, he pulled himself to his full height. "No matter what sort of task it is, we'll do it."

Anwen's jowls flapped as she nodded eagerly in

agreement. "We'll solve your Wolf Father's tasks, no problem."

Astrus let out a long breath. "All right. This way."

As Astrus started deeper into the cave, Cavall gave a sharp bark to get the people's attention.

"Now what are those dogs doing?" Bedivere sighed.

"They want us to follow them," Arthur exclaimed. "We must be close indeed." He helped Lucan to his feet. "Can you keep going just a little bit? It can't be far now. We have to have faith in Cavall."

Cavall's heart swelled. Before, when Arthur had said that, he'd felt guilty about wanting to find the cave for his own ends. Well, now Cavall intended to help the people find the Holy Grail, if only to help Lucan. "You can trust me," he said over his shoulder, to the people who were counting on him. "I promise you can trust me."

Lucan walked leaning heavily on Arthur, while Bedivere followed behind holding the horses' reins. They remained several paces behind the dogs, silent except for the sound of their boots echoing off the walls and Lucan's occasional coughing.

The cave stretched and stretched. If it weren't for the crystals, they would have needed torches because it would be very dark in here. As it was, it grew brighter and brighter the deeper into the cave they wandered. The moss and grass near the entrance disappeared quickly, and soon there was nothing but glowing rock on all sides, still blue, but also in colors Cavall couldn't see.

He paused to catch a reflection of himself in one of the larger crystals. It made his nose look bigger than his face, but if he looked long enough, he could just make out images inside. Images that moved. Two wolf pups lay curled around each other in the shelter of a cave, shivering as rain poured down outside. For some reason, Cavall knew that they were all alone in the world, except for each other. One of the pups had a patch of white fur on her forehead.

"You can see it, can't you?" Astrus asked.

Cavall startled. He thought she'd be up at the front, leading the way. He hadn't realized she'd circled around behind him. "It?" he asked.

"The prophecy," she answered, as if it were obvious. "It's

different for everyone who looks into the crystals. Some see their own future. Some see things that won't occur for a long, long time, or things that happened long ago. Some don't see anything at all."

Cavall looked back into the crystal, but the images were gone. "What do you see?" he asked.

She looked past him, into the crystal. "I see an empty cave. I see a time when we guardians are no longer needed to protect the treasures here. But I don't know if that's my future or something a long, long time from now."

"And what does your sister see?"

"I don't know. She won't tell me." She was silent a moment, staring at whatever revealed itself to her in that crystal.

Seeing the two wolf pups in his own vision, Cavall felt an odd compulsion to ask, "Why does she hate people?"

Astrus tore her eyes from the crystal, aiming them somewhere on the ground. Her ears flattened against her head. "A hunter killed our mother."

Cavall didn't know what to say to that. He remembered his own mother, how kind and warm she'd been. If she'd been killed by a person, he might not be so quick to trust them either. "I'm sorry," he said at last.

Astrus shook her head. "It happened a long time ago."

"Hey, you two!" Anwen hollered from up ahead.

It felt like he and Astrus had been alone for a moment, but then the world came rushing back. He wanted to ask her more questions, but she shook her entire body, as if trying to dry herself, and trotted to catch up with the others.

Cavall followed behind her, feeling incredibly sad.

He parted between the people, who had come to a stop for some reason. Only when he caught sight of the dogs did he understand why. Anwen and Gless stood staring up at an enormous boulder sitting in the middle of the path. As high as the cave's ceiling and as wide as the walls, the boulder blocked the path tight. On either side of it, someone as small as Anwen *might* have been able to stick their nose into the crevice, but certainly nothing more than that. They couldn't go any farther.

"What is this?" Anwen huffed.

"It's the first test," Astrus said. "The test of strength."

Gless strode forward. He might have been carved out of the same stone as the cave for how rigid his posture was. "I'll take this test. I think we can all agree that I'm the strongest here."

"Now wait just a moment!" Anwen pushed her way in front of him. "You may be strong, but that doesn't mean you're fit to take this test."

"What is the test?" Cavall asked, nervously looking at his injured paw. He suspected it wasn't going to be easy, getting into the cave, but he didn't like the idea of any one of them putting themselves in even more danger.

"There's only one way to clear the path for the test of strength." Astrus closed her eyes and took a deep breath, as if preparing herself to give them bad news. "You have to move it."

"We have to *move* that thing?" Cavall didn't see how it was possible. The boulder was the size of a house!

A moment of incredulous silence followed.

"I'm the pack leader," Anwen said. "I should be the one to take this test."

Gless snorted, and she shot him a warning glare.

She turned her scrutiny back to the boulder, as if sizing it up. Her droopy eyes roved it up and down.

Then she pulled her lips back into an almost human-looking smile. A determined gleam shone in her eye as she trotted up to the boulder, lifted her head, and addressed it. "I'm here to take your test, cave," she announced. Her bark echoed off the closed-in walls. "Do your worst. I am not afraid. Because one way or another, I *am* moving you."

CHAPTER 15

NWEN LAID HER FOREHEAD AGAINST THE boulder. Dug her stubby legs into the ground. And began pushing.

"What are you doing?" Gless scoffed. "That rock's immovable. And even if it weren't, there's no way someone as small as *you* would be able to move it."

"Well," Anwen answered, still pushing, "the only other option is to give up. And that's *not* an option."

She shoved and heaved until her shoulders strained. But even then, she only muttered darkly under her breath and didn't stop.

"You're only going to hurt yourself," Gless said.

"Let me help you," Cavall said. He looked to Astrus. "Is that allowed?"

"I don't think the Wolf Father would care," she replied. "He was never keen on rules to begin with. But I think he would frown on *me* helping you."

Cavall supposed that was permission enough. He joined Anwen's side and, laying his head against the rock, lent her his strength to move it.

It felt like . . . well, it felt like trying to move a boulder. No matter how he clawed at the ground or pushed with all his strength, the thing just wouldn't move. Anwen wasn't giving up, though, so he wouldn't either. He gritted his teeth against the pain in his wounded paw and continued to shove.

He was startled when he felt a presence by his side. "You're both crazy," Gless said as he took a position next to Cavall. The muscles in his chest and shoulders bulged as he began to push along with them.

The three of them worked together.

"What are they doing now?" Bedivere's voice carried down the tunnel.

"Trying to move the boulder blocking our way," Arthur answered, and a moment later, Cavall felt his person's presence right next to him as well. "They haven't led us astray yet," he announced as he braced himself against the rock. "We should help them." And he began helping as well. Lucan joined in next to Gless, and now they had five bodies working together. It was enough that Cavall began to think they actually had a chance of moving it.

Astrus sat by Lucan's side. "Come on!" she called to them. "You can do it! I know you can!"

Cavall dug in with renewed energy. His legs trembled, especially the wounded one, and his neck ached. Above him, Arthur's face grew dark and the veins in his forehead stood out. Bedivere smelled strongly of sweat, and even Gless grunted at the strain of it. But Anwen worked the hardest, her entire body shaking with the effort of moving that rock. Her breath came in ragged gasps, when she wasn't muttering angrily to herself. Her nails scrabbled against the ground. Foamy drool dripped down her jowls, but she didn't relent in the slightest.

They worked for what felt like forever, until Bedivere

finally stepped back with an exhausted sigh and clutched his knees. "It's no use," he said. "That thing just won't budge."

Arthur stepped back as well and wiped his forehead. "Doesn't look like we're making any progress at all," he agreed. "In any event, I need a break."

Gless let out an irritated sigh and sat back on his haunches. "This is useless," he panted. His tongue hung out of his mouth. "Even the people know you're being foolish." Gless went to join them as they drank from their water skins. If Gless couldn't move this thing, using all of his strength, what hope did they have?

Anwen wasn't giving up, though, so Cavall continued as well. Until he pressed too hard on his wounded paw and leapt back with a yelp. Anwen paused only briefly to look up at him. "Are you all right?"

Cavall licked his paw. "I'm sorry, Anwen, but I think the others are right. There's no way to move that thing." He nodded to the boulder, which had not moved even a hair's breadth since they'd started. "Maybe we can find another way around. Maybe there's another entrance or—"

"No," Anwen snapped, and went straight back to work. "We don't have time for any of that. This is the quickest way in." She grunted as she continued her efforts.

"Your head will give in before the rock does," Gless called.

Anwen ignored him, too intent on her task.

"He's right," Cavall said, leaning in close to her. "You're going to hurt yourself if you keep—"

"I'm not quitting." She stopped and glared up at him, daring him to challenge her. If Cavall had forgotten why she was the leader of the hunt, he was quickly reminded now. "If Astrus says this rock needs to move so that we can keep going, then I will move it. That's that."

Her nostrils flared angrily, but Cavall didn't argue with her anymore. *Couldn't* really argue anymore. She had her own way of doing things, and he wasn't going to change her mind in any case. He knew what it was like to be so single-minded in an objective, especially when it came to protecting Arthur, but where he would try to find another solution when the first failed, Anwen preferred to meet things head-on.

Anwen went back to her task.

No sooner had she placed her head against the boulder than the whole cave began to shake. Bedivere and Arthur shot to their feet as bits of loose rock came raining down on them. Even Gless looked around in bewilderment.

A horrendous grating sound filled the tunnel, and all eyes turned to the boulder as it slowly, slowly began to move forward. It groaned as it went. Everyone stared in awe as it rolled, like an enormous ball, gradually gaining momentum as it went, until it jerked, teetered for a moment, and then fell down with a resounding *thud*.

Everyone waited for the cave to stop shaking before running to see. There was a massive hole just behind where the boulder had been. A hole just the right size for the boulder to fit in to bridge the gap. Beyond lay the newly opened tunnel.

Anwen stood with her jaw hanging open, eyes comically wide.

Astrus licked Lucan's face and jumped excitedly to her feet. "You look surprised that you passed the first test," she called out to Anwen.

"But I . . . I didn't . . ." Anwen shook her head, spraying slaver everywhere. "That thing just moved on its own!"

"Because you passed the test," Astrus explained. "The test of strength is a measure of your resolve and persistence. The Wolf Father was never someone who valued physical strength. But the strength to carry on against all odds, even in the face of the impossible . . . well, that's something he wanted in the ones who would prove themselves worthy of his treasure."

Anwen puffed out her chest. "Well, then . . ." She strutted over the boulder—more of a bridge now. "Like taking a nap. Let's pass these last two tests and get on with it, shall we?"

Gless rolled his eyes.

Arthur and Bedivere helped Lucan to his feet, and together they all continued down the tunnel.

Here the crystals were smaller but more numerous, and their light reflected off one another. As they crossed over the boulder, Cavall noticed strange symbols had been carved into the rock. Cavall couldn't tell what they meant, though he thought he saw one that matched the rune on his collar. He stopped to peer into the smaller crystals, just to check if he still saw the same image. He did. The two wolf pups curled around each other. He now knew for sure they were Astrus and her sister, Gudrun.

He looked over at Astrus, trotting by his side. Her eyes were wide and bright, and she seemed happy they had passed the first test.

"Why are you helping us?" He didn't even realize he'd said that out loud until she turned to give him a curious look. "I mean . . . why don't you hate people like your sister does?"

Astrus tilted her head toward the ceiling. She seemed to think for a long time.

"I . . . used to hate humans—I mean people, too," she admitted. "I thought they were all evil. I thought they only wanted to kill and destroy. And . . . when I fell in that trap, I thought for sure that the first human to find me would kill me as well. But that man . . . Lucan . . . he helped me. He didn't have to. I thought maybe he was just a special human, but after all we've been through the past few days, seeing the way you and your person interact, I've begun to think . . . maybe there are other humans who aren't bad."

"There *are* people who are bad," Cavall said, thinking of Mordred and Morgana, "but there are many, many more who aren't. I used to think that all wolves were evil, but after meeting you, I've begun to think that wolves are like people. They're all different."

Astrus made a small noise of agreement. Cavall wondered if she was thinking just as much about what he'd said as he was thinking about what she'd said. They walked along in silence, listening to Gless and Anwen argue over who would take the next test.

CHAPTER 16

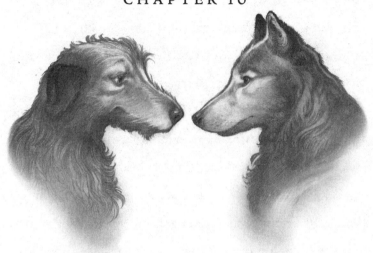

S THEY WALKED, THE SYMBOLS ON THE WALL became more frequent, forming long lines that ran under and over the crystals. Cavall couldn't look at them too closely, because they played tricks on his eyes. It almost seemed like the runes were moving. The sound of wind whistled through the tunnel, though there was no breeze. Occasionally, Lucan would cough, but nobody spoke.

The tunnel curved, and as they rounded the corner, they came upon a wall of solid crystal blocking their path. It was smooth and shimmery, almost like a mirror, and as they approached, the reflection of three dogs, three people, and a wolf came up to meet them.

"Let me guess," Anwen said. "The second test."

"The test of honesty," Astrus said with a nod.

"Honesty?" Anwen grunted. "I seem to recall that one of your Wolf Father's many names was Lie-Smith. Why would someone called Lie-Smith care about honesty?"

Astrus shrugged. "I guess someone named Lie-Smith would be pretty good at telling if someone is lying or not. I think it's best if just one of you took this test, though."

"Why's that?" Gless asked.

Astrus looked at him as if the answer were obvious. "Because it's hard enough to get *one* person to tell the truth."

Anwen snorted. "In that case, there's no contest. Cavall should take this one."

"You think so?" Cavall asked nervously.

Gless nodded solemnly. "You're the only one here who's honest to a fault."

Cavall wasn't sure what that meant—it sounded like a compliment that wasn't really a compliment—but if he had their trust, then he would do it. He approached the crystal warily. His distorted reflection stared back at him, hazy and indistinct in the crystal.

"Who are you?" a voice said. It rang out through the cave, and yet seemed to be coming from inside him. He couldn't quite explain it. Just like he couldn't explain why it sounded like *his* voice.

"I'm . . . Cavall," he answered uncertainly. "Who are *you?*"

He blinked in surprise as his reflection sat back on its haunches, even though Cavall hadn't moved at all. "You know who I am."

"Are you . . . the cave?" Cavall asked, remembering what Astrus had told him earlier about the cave "speaking."

His reflection gave a curt nod. "You wish to take the test of honesty, to see if you are worthy to pass?"

"I do."

"Then you must answer my questions, and answer them truthfully."

"I will."

His reflection stood. "First of all, I am curious. How did you learn of the Crystal Cave?"

"From Merlin," Cavall answered.

"Merlin," the voice repeated in a hushed whisper. "Is *that* the name he goes by in these lands?"

It seemed to be speaking more to itself than to him, but Cavall answered anyway. "If you mean Merlin the wizard, that's the only name I know him by."

His reflection blinked, as if being pulled back from a faraway memory. It reminded Cavall of the look Merlin himself had worn when he'd spoken of the cave.

"My next question," it went on. "Why have you come here?"

"I've come to find the Holy Grail."

His reflection shook its head. "No, you have not."

The response took him by surprise. He flapped his jaw a few times, trying to understand what it meant.

"Yes, I have," he managed to finally get out. "I came here because I need the Holy Grail to heal my friend."

His reflection chuckled. "Is that truly what you want, in your heart of hearts?"

"Of course it is," Cavall answered, growing angrier. "I want to save my friend. All my friends. I want to protect them and make sure nothing bad happens to them."

"That's true," his reflection said. "You do wish to

protect your friends, but in your deepest heart, you desire something else besides the Holy Grail."

"I . . . ," Cavall began weakly.

His reflection turned its head away. "You have failed my test, Cavall."

"No!" Cavall jumped at the reflection. "Please, let me try again. I'll answer truthfully this time, I promise." But the reflection had become just that—a reflection again. It jumped back at him, moved right or left when he did, raised its paw to mimic him. Whatever power had given it its own life was now gone.

Cavall sank back, stunned. He sat there for a long moment, trying to work out what had just happened.

"What's going on over there?" Anwen called.

Cavall sighed and stood and walked back to the others. "I failed," he told them in a small voice. It hurt to admit. He wanted the Grail, if only to save Lucan, but deep down, he still wanted Gelert's Wish more. The cave had known, and now they would never be able to pass. He hadn't just failed the test, he'd failed everyone here. They'd trusted him, and he'd proven to be unworthy of their trust.

"I'll take the test," Gless said.

Astrus studied the blocked path with a furrowed brow. "Well, the cave won't allow anyone in who's unworthy . . . so I suppose you can try as many times as you like."

Gless brushed roughly past her. "Then allow me to try."

Everyone watched, breaths held, as Gless approached the crystal wall. A distorted reflection came up to meet him. "Who are you?" it asked in an eerie voice that whistled like the wind through the tunnel.

"My name is Glessic," Gless announced.

"And you wish to take my test?"

"I do."

"Very well. Why have you come here?"

"To find the Holy Grail."

"Why?"

Gless shifted from paw to paw nervously. "To heal my person, Prince Mordred Pendragon."

Cavall blinked in surprise. Had Gless actually admitted . . . ?

"He lies ill in Camelot," Gless continued, "after being thrown from his horse by a dark creature he summoned to attack Arthur Pendragon, his father. But . . . he miscast the spell from Morgana's book . . . I tried to warn him not to . . . and it turned on him during the hunt."

"Impossible," Anwen muttered. "You mean to tell me that garmr thing has been chasing us this whole time because *Mordred* was trying to play sorcerer?"

Cavall realized he'd suspected it all along. What he hadn't suspected was that Gless had joined them on this quest for Mordred's sake. He always insisted he didn't care, but *that* was the lie.

"He needs the Holy Grail to survive." Gless's voice grew smaller and smaller. "Please, I don't want Mordred to die." He lowered his head, although the reflection did not. "I . . . I've grown somewhat fond of him."

In that moment, Cavall's heart ached for his brother.

Gless's reflection regarded him for a long while. Then nodded. "You speak the truth. You may enter."

Everyone, including the people, watched in wonder as the wall became more and more transparent, until it was so clear you could see through to the other side. Something glimmered from farther down the tunnel, something brighter than even the crystals all around them. Could that be the inner chamber?

Arthur stepped forward hesitantly and reached out a

hand. His fingers passed right through where the wall had been. He stared in wonder for a moment, then burst into a hearty laugh. "I'm not sure what you've done, Gless, but you've certainly done it." He patted Gless on the rump, and Gless tensed at the gesture. "Mordred would be proud."

Gless's tail thumped exactly once.

"Well, I'll be." Anwen shook her head. "If you'd told me *Gless* would be the one to pass the honesty test . . ." She looked guiltily at Cavall. "Sorry, Cavall. I just meant . . ."

"No, you're right," Cavall admitted. "Gless told the cave what he wanted from the bottom of his heart, and I . . . didn't." He hung his head, unable to face any of them. Least of all the people, who didn't even know he'd almost cost them their chance of finding the Holy Grail altogether.

He looked up when he felt a presence by his side. "Don't be sad," Astrus said, licking his muzzle. "All that matters is that the way is open now."

Cavall looked into her wide eyes, warm where her sister's were cold. She was right. He'd nearly cost them this chance because he'd lost track of what they were really here for. Maybe he wasn't worthy of entering the cave at all, but now that their goal was within reach, he couldn't stop to feel sorry for himself. Not when others were still depending on him.

A gleaming crystal archway stood over the entrance, engraved with intricate, intertwining lines and more runes. At the top, where the arch curved, the two mirror-image wolves met, nose to nose. Their gemstone eyes seemed to watch the party as they approached.

Anwen glanced around. "I thought you said there were *three* test—"

She stopped short as a figure appeared in their path, silhouetted against the light from the cave. A figure with shaggy fur and pointed ears, one of them missing a big chunk. The scent of fallen leaves washed over them, and Cavall recognized the smell of wolf. Gudrun, Astrus's sister. "So we meet again, human lover."

CHAPTER 17

STRUS STEPPED FORWARD TO MEET HER SISTER. "Let them pass, Gudrun. They've proven themselves worthy."

"Only on two of the tests," Gudrun sneered.

"Are you going to stop us?" Gless growled, hackles raised.

This time, however, Gudrun didn't react in kind. "I'm not going to stop you," she said. "I've been watching you since you entered the cave, and since it seems you're determined not to leave until you've found what you're looking for, I've decided to help you."

"Really?" Cavall asked incredulously.

Gless narrowed his eyes in suspicion. "Why would you do that? You were willing to fight us last time to keep us from getting the Grail."

She narrowed her eyes back. Her tail flicked back and forth in agitation. "Consider this an extension of the test of honesty." She leveled her pale blue eyes at them, at Cavall in particular. "What do you plan to do once you've found what you're looking for?"

"We're going to heal our friend," Cavall said, nodding toward Lucan. "And then we're going back to Camelot to heal . . ." Our other friend? Mordred was certainly not his friend. "Someone else."

"So you're going to leave, then?"

"Yes."

"And will you come back? To the Crystal Cave, I mean."

"I don't see why we would need to," Anwen answered.

"So you're going to leave and never come back?"

"I suppose so," Cavall said.

"Do you promise?" Gudrun barked sharply, surprising them all. "Do you promise, when you have what you want, that you'll go back to where you came from and leave me and my sister in peace?"

Cavall looked to his friends. *He* was willing to make a compromise, but what of the others?

"We promise," Gless said, surprising him. "But only if you promise not to get in our way."

Gudrun curled her lip. "We understand each other, then." She turned around and disappeared behind the archway, only to return a brief moment later, now with something in her mouth. Something with two bits of dangling leather hanging off it—the rune stone collar! She cantered back to them and dropped it at Cavall's feet.

"That's the first thing you want, right?"

"Thank you," Cavall said.

She flattened her ears against her head. "It wasn't even worth stealing in the first place."

Cavall picked up the stone by the leather cord and trotted over to Arthur. "What have you got there, boy?" He took the stone from her mouth. "Why, it's your collar. Now, how did you manage to lose that?" He shook his head. "Come here. We'll get this back on you."

Cavall leaned against him as he tied the bit of leather around his neck. Ah, that was much better.

"Hurry up!" Gudrun called. She turned and stalked into the cave. Everyone else followed behind her.

The inside of the cavern loomed larger than the great hall back at Camelot, perhaps larger than the entire castle itself. It stretched up so high that Cavall couldn't see the ceiling, even when he craned his neck. Every last bit of wall not covered with glowing crystals was covered with all manner of shiny things: golden jewelry, crystal orbs, marble statues, metal armor so heavy and elaborate that Cavall couldn't imagine anyone actually wearing it. There were also things like books and furniture, smelling of distant places and ages.

For a long time, everyone just stared, trying to take it all in.

"Truly . . . a treasure trove . . . fit for a king," Lucan gasped.

"Hush," Bedivere chastised. "Don't speak." He helped Lucan onto a piece of furniture that couldn't decide if it wanted to be a chair or a sofa. Whatever it was, it had elaborately carved legs that looked like animals Cavall had never seen before, and smelled of pungent smoke from a faraway land.

"We'll bring you the Grail when we find it," Arthur said.

Bedivere looked around the cavern again. "How will we find it among all of . . . this?"

"We search, I suppose."

The people began sorting through the treasures. Metal clanged as objects were tossed to the side.

"Which one of these things is the Holy Grail?" Cavall asked Astrus and Gudrun.

Astrus looked to Gudrun. "You know where everything is better than I do."

"That's because *you've* never been interested in being a real guardian." Gudrun snorted.

"It's not how I've ever wanted to spend my life," Astrus shot back. "It's not fun staying near the cave all the time, never getting to see the world or meet anyone."

"But we've always had each other." Gudrun turned to her, pale eyes wide and filled with a vulnerability Cavall hadn't noticed before. "Isn't that enough?"

Astrus didn't answer, just stared back. A silent conversation seemed to pass between the two sisters. Cavall shifted uncomfortably. It felt like he was intruding on something private.

"Ahem," Anwen said, drawing their attention back. "The Grail?"

"Ah . . . right." Gudrun seemed almost embarrassed by the subtle drooping of her tail and ears. "I . . . actually . . . don't know *which* one is the Holy Grail."

"I'm not sure I know what a grail even is," Astrus said.

"It's a fancy cup that humans drink out of," Gudrun said bitingly. It reminded Cavall of something Gless would say, correcting one of his mistakes. "But it could be anywhere." She craned her neck high. "It could even be up there."

Cavall really hoped not.

"Gudrun . . . ," Astrus said quietly, still looking embarrassed after her sister's sharp comment. "Why did you steal their rune stone again?"

Gudrun gave a dramatic sigh and rolled her eyes. "Because its magic felt like the Wolf Father's magic. I already *said* I was sorry."

"I just meant . . ." Astrus scratched idly at the ground.

"The Wolf Father stole the Grail from the Fisher King. And the Fisher King is one of the Old Fay, like the Wolf Father. So I was thinking . . . maybe . . . if your rune was made with Old Fay magic . . ."

"It might be able to show us which one is the Holy Grail," Cavall finished. "The way we were planning to find the cave in the first place."

Gudrun's nostrils flared. "I suppose it might work." She sounded doubtful.

"It's our best chance." Gless's deep voice startled Cavall as his brother came to stand next to him. In fact, everyone seemed startled, staring at him. Gless only lifted his nose in the air. "If I thought I could find it faster by searching on my own, I would."

"Still keeping up the glory hound act?" Anwen chided him. "We all heard what you told the cave back there. You really *are* worried about Mordred."

Gless kicked at the ground. "Can you please wait to humiliate me until after we find the Grail?"

"Fine," Anwen said, waggling her eyebrows. "But I'm going to remind you of this every time you step out of line from now on."

Gless grumbled something under his breath, then looked hopefully to Cavall.

They all did.

They were counting on him again. He couldn't let them down this time. He closed his eyes, blocking out the thousand glittering things around him, and tuned his ears to the stone on his collar.

And there it was. Not a noise, exactly, so maybe it wasn't his ears that were "hearing" it. But a soft, rhythmic beat, like that of a heart. He opened his eyes and began forward, and the rhythm became more intense. So he followed it.

A pattering of footsteps followed behind him, but the farther into the cave he went, the more the stone drowned them out.

They circled around a mound of gold. Amid all the coins, Cavall noticed pieces of jewelry: necklaces, rings, crowns, bracelets. A few stood out because of their shining blue gems. He wondered if they had stories behind them, just like the Holy Grail. He wondered if everything in here—the armor, the furniture, the weapons, statues, masks—had a story of its own.

So many stories in one place. Drudwyn would love it.

Cavall led them onward. The stone's beat grew stronger.

Up ahead lay a door with a brass ring, like those found on cabinets, built into the very crystal of the cavern's wall. A simple symbol was carved into its dark wood, looking a little like a left-facing arrow. Cavall couldn't tell what it meant, but it reminded him of the symbol on his rune, which was leading him right to this very spot.

"In there?" Anwen asked as Cavall came to a stop in front of it. "How are we supposed to open that?"

"Perhaps we should tell the people," Cavall suggested.

Gless pushed his way forward. "We don't need the people." He studied the door's brass ring for a moment before taking it between his teeth and giving a sharp tug.

The door did not budge.

Gless tried again, to the same result, so he spat out the ring and began clawing at the wood with his paws. "Stupid thing," he growled. "I'll tear it down if I have to."

"You can try all you want," Gudrun said, "but my guess is that door's locked with the Wolf Father's magic."

Gless whirled on her. "Then how do we *unlock* it?"

The symbol on the door began to glow, and a hushed

voice said, "To unlock my greatest treasure, you must first answer my riddle."

"*That's* the third test?" Anwen cried. "A riddle?"

"It's the test of knowledge," Gudrun said.

"The Wolf Father loved riddles," Astrus agreed.

Cavall gave his friends an uncertain look. Between Anwen and Gless, they surely must be smart enough to answer the Wolf Father's riddle. Though Cavall wasn't sure how much help *he* would be.

"*I'll* answer it," Gless said. "Give me your stupid riddle."

The voice let out a raspy chuckle, like the crinkling of dead leaves, and began:

"It soars without wings, it runs without feet.
It changes with time, yet keeps steady beat.
Some come made of stone, others of gold,
Some are quite soft, others are cold.
It breaks, it aches, and heavy or light,
Everyone's leads them and tells them what's right."

A moment passed where nobody spoke, simply taking in the words.

Gless was the first to speak. "A compass," he pronounced, without a hint of doubt in his voice.

"How do you figure that?" Anwen asked.

"It's obvious," he explained. "Compasses lead people where they need to go, they can be made out of a variety of material and come in all shapes and sizes."

"Then what's all that about wings and legs?"

"Silly nonsense, obviously."

"No," Cavall said. All eyes turned to him, but he didn't flinch. He was too busy thinking. "Soaring, running, beating . . ." Those all sounded like something that moved. That moved quickly? An animal? Was there an animal made out of stone? He'd seen an animal made out of shadow, so maybe . . . no, not if everyone *had* one. Cavall thought about himself. What did he have that moved sometimes quickly and sometimes slowly? And was his made of gold or stone?

With a sudden clarity, it came to him.

"It's a heart." He felt his own pounding up in his throat. "The answer is a heart."

Everyone looked at him with mixed expressions of shock.

"Everyone has a heart," he explained. Stone. That had been the final clue. "Even Mordred."

"Congratulations, Cavall," the voice answered. "You've finally earned the right to my treasures. Next time, remember to be honest with your friends and yourself from the beginning." And with a click, the door swung open.

CHAPTER 18

ON THE OTHER SIDE OF THE DOOR, IN A LITTLE alcove carved from the crystal, sat a single cup. Shiny and clean, yes, but not remarkable in any other way. It looked like any of the hundreds of cups the people drank from back at the castle.

"*That's* the Holy Grail?" Gless scoffed.

"Yes," Cavall answered, just as surely as he'd answered the Wolf Father's riddle. He just knew. "That's the Holy Grail."

He twisted his head to reach into the alcove and grab the Grail's handle with his mouth. It tasted the way metal

184

smelled—like dark soil and just a coppery hint of blood—but he was too eager to be bothered that much. Something heavy rattled around inside the cup.

From the other side of the cave, Lucan coughed again, and Bedivere cried, "Hold on just a little longer."

Cavall wrenched around quickly, stumbling as he forgot about his wounded paw. The rattling thing went flying out and hit the ground with a dull *thud*.

"What is that?" Anwen went to investigate, nose sniffing.

"No time for that," Cavall said. "We have to get the Grail to Lucan right away." He fought back against the wave of pain in his paw and hurried off in the direction of the people's voices. "This way!" he called to the others. "I want them to know that I didn't find it on my own."

He found Arthur searching in a pile of golden coins, so intent that he only looked up when Cavall barreled into him, nearly knocking him over.

"Cavall, what—?" he sputtered, his voice sharp with displeasure. His angry expression gave way to hope at seeing what Cavall laid at his feet. "Is that . . . ?" He bent to pick it up and examined it in his hands as Anwen, Gless, Astrus, and Gudrun all arrived at the scene as well. "Is this the Holy Grail, Cavall? Did *you* find it?" He looked at them all, dog and wolf, and then turned his head and called out, "Bedivere!"

Bedivere came running, and Arthur ran to meet him. "Have you found it?"

"The animals did."

They all hurried back to Lucan's side. He had grown even paler while they were gone and was breathing so heavily he couldn't even speak, though he looked like he wanted to.

"Hurry," Arthur ordered, "uncap the water skin and pour some water."

Bedivere did so with shaking hands. Some of the water sloshed out, but most of it went into the Grail. Arthur's hands also shook as he lifted it to Lucan's mouth.

"Here. Drink."

Lucan did. His throat bobbed as the water went down. After a few gulps, Arthur pulled the Grail back.

"Now," Arthur breathed, "we wait to see if this truly is the Holy Grail."

The words were barely out of his mouth when Lucan gasped loudly and clutched at his ribs. Bedivere was by his side in an instant. "What is it? What's wrong?"

Lucan lifted his shirt to reveal a dark bruise that covered nearly half his side from where he had smashed against the tree during the garmr's attack. Before their eyes, it slowly shrank and faded. "It . . . is a strange feeling," he gasped. With a cracking sound, his ribs took their proper shape.

Everyone, people, dogs, and wolves alike, stared in amazement.

Bedivere grasped Lucan's shoulders and Arthur clasped his hands in front of him, the way Gwen had when she'd told everyone to pray for Mordred. "Truly a miracle," he whispered.

Lucan started to sit up, and Bedivere helped him. "How are you feeling?"

"Better than I have in my entire life." Lucan laughed.

Bedivere threw his arms around his brother and gave him a hug so hard that Cavall worried he might break his ribs again.

Arthur placed a hand on Cavall's head. Then he turned to the wolf sisters. "My friends," he began. Both of them looked up in surprise at being addressed directly by a human. "You have done so much for us today. The Knights of the Round Table are forever in your debt."

He drew Excalibur out. The wolves flinched, but he only stuck the bladed end into the ground and knelt, lowering his head.

"I, Arthur Pendragon, king of England, will forbid the hunting of wolves in my kingdom from this day forth, in your honor. No longer will a knight of the Round Table bring harm to a wolf, save in self-defense. This I promise."

Silence reigned.

Astrus and Gudrun stood rooted in place, looking unsure of how to respond.

"It's a lovely vow," Bedivere said at last, "but I don't think they understand you."

It startled Cavall when Gudrun stepped forward first. She kept her head low, but her eyes stayed fixed on Arthur's. He breathed heavily through his nose, as if unsure what to expect from her. Bedivere kept one hand on Lucan's shoulder and the other on the hilt of his sword, if only halfheartedly. Gudrun's eyes flicked to him for a moment, then back to Arthur. She took one final step so that they were nose to nose, and then she licked his face.

Arthur sputtered and laughed. At the noise, Astrus darted forward and joined her sister. She licked Arthur's face, then ran to Lucan's side and licked *his* face. She even jumped up and tried to lick Bedivere's face, and he gave her a light push to keep her off him. He wore a smile, though, as Arthur got back to his feet and sheathed Excalibur.

"Bedivere, if I may have the Grail again . . ."

Bedivere handed it over, and Arthur beckoned to Cavall. "And you . . ." He knelt down and held out the Grail, half-filled with water. "Here," he said. "Your paw is still wounded."

Cavall looked at him warily. How could he explain that he didn't deserve to drink from the Holy Grail? That he'd started this quest for selfish reasons and had almost ruined everything for all of them?

Arthur knitted his brow in concern and held the Grail out again, sloshing a bit of water over the side. "It's all right, Cavall. You can drink."

Cavall lowered his head.

"What's the matter?" Arthur set the Grail down and took Cavall's head in his hands, gently rubbing his ears. "Please, won't you drink? You are still wounded from saving my life earlier. I hate to see you hurt."

"I hate to see you hurt, too," Cavall said, though he knew Arthur wouldn't understand him. He wasn't worthy to drink from the Grail, but if it would make Arthur happy, he'd do it.

When Arthur held out the Grail again, he dipped his nose into the cup and lapped at the water while Arthur patted his side. "There you go," he said in a hushed tone. "If any hound has ever earned the right to drink from the Holy Grail, it is you."

Cavall still doubted it, but he was just happy that Arthur was happy.

Lucan was right; it was a strange feeling to be healed so quickly. The bite marks on Cavall's paw closed up and grew over with new fur, but he couldn't see it until Arthur knelt down and unwound the bandages. Sure enough, his paw was completely healed. He romped around a few paces to test it out. It held his weight fine, and there was no hint of the previous pain.

Arthur laughed, then bent his head and rested his forehead against the lip of the Grail. Then he began crying.

Cavall was taken aback at the odd shift, and he hurried over to lean against his person, hoping to ease whatever pain he was in. Arthur ran an absentminded hand over Cavall's head. "Forgive me," he murmured. "I'm overcome. We found the Holy Grail. We can save Mordred."

Mordred. He had saved Lucan, but in doing so, he'd also saved Mordred. Somehow, he couldn't make himself regret it. Maybe it was because Lucan was worth saving more than Mordred was worth *not* saving. Or maybe it was because Arthur was happy again. Or maybe it was because he now knew Gless actually cared about Mordred, in his strange Gless-like way.

He felt Astrus standing by his side.

Or maybe, he thought, Arthur had been right all along. Maybe there truly was nobody who was not worth saving.

"I picked this up for you," Astrus said, dropping something at his feet. It was a stone, about the size of a person's fist, dark and smooth, with the image of a dog's paw etched in intricate lines and a bunch of other symbols Cavall couldn't understand but recognized from books. "It fell out of the Grail. I think the Wolf Father wanted you to have it."

"What is it?" Cavall asked, though he thought he already knew.

"It's what you've been looking for." Astrus nudged it closer to him. "It's Gelert's Wish."

CHAPTER 19

"HAT NOW?" BEDIVERE ASKED AS HE HELPED
Lucan to his feet. This time, however, Lucan
shooed him away.

"Now?" Arthur said. "We ride back to Camelot as
quickly as we can."

"With that beast still out there?"

Bedivere was right. The garmr would be waiting for
them when they tried to leave the cave. But now Cavall
could warn them about why it was chasing them, and who
had sent it. They could make a plan, together.

His heartbeat thundered in his ears as he carried

Gelert's Wish over to Arthur. Did he deserve to have this second chance to have his heart's desire? Well, as long as he was willing to give Mordred and Gless a second chance, perhaps he could do the same for himself. He just had to make sure he didn't break the Wolf Father's newfound trust in him.

He dropped the stone at his person's feet. Arthur looked up from his intense studying of the Grail and gave Cavall a quizzical look.

"Can you understand me, Arthur?"

Arthur didn't respond, only patted his head.

Cavall frowned. He'd touched the stone. Shouldn't that make the Wish work? *Oh*, he realized, *maybe I need to be touching it* when *I try to talk to him*. He set his paw on the shard.

"How about now?"

Arthur cocked his head in confusion. Cavall's heart soared, but Arthur only knelt down again and said, "What have you brought me, boy?" He picked it up and read the symbols out loud. "'May no man ever lose his friend as I have lost mine. May the power of this Wish bring understanding between beast and man.'"

"What's that?" Lucan asked.

"Something Cavall brought me."

All right, perhaps Arthur needed to touch it as well. That made sense, since it would be the two of them talking to each other.

"That's Gelert's Wish," Cavall explained. "It lets us talk to each other."

Arthur continued to study the stone. "Someone put a lot of work into this inscription, but I doubt it's worth much on its own."

Cavall was growing frustrated now. Maybe . . . maybe they both needed to touch it at the same time? He reached his paw into Arthur's hand. "Please, can you understand me now?"

Arthur shook his head. "It seems you're fond of this thing, in any case. Fine, I'll bring it with us. You deserve to have your own choice of treasure, even if I do not understand your fascination with it." Arthur stood, Grail in one hand and stone in the other. He did not answer Cavall's question.

What was going on?

The people began to gather up their packs. Cavall scrambled back to Astrus. "It didn't work."

Astrus furrowed her brow, but Gudrun simply snorted dismissively. "That's not our problem. I helped you find what you were looking for. Now you need to uphold your promise and leave."

"But, Gudrun," Astrus said, "the garmr is still after them."

"And that is not our problem either," Gudrun sniffed. "As far as I'm concerned, the sooner they're gone, the sooner things can go back to normal."

Astrus glowered at her sister, then puffed up her chest and stepped toward Cavall. "I'll at least escort you back to the entrance. Maybe we can figure out how to get Gelert's Wish to work on the way."

Cavall lowered his head in gratitude. "Thank you."

"Astrus," Gudrun warned. "You don't owe them anything."

"Then maybe I'm helping them because I *want* to," Astrus said back. "Maybe I don't want things to 'go back to normal.' Did you ever think about that?"

Gudrun's eyes widened in surprise, and Cavall thought he might have seen hurt there as well. "Astrus . . ."

"You know I love you, Gudrun," Astrus said, and there was hurt in her eyes as well, "but I don't want to live the rest of my life here, waiting for the Wolf Father or the First Guardian to come back."

Gudrun's shocked expression turned into a deep scowl. "I only helped them in the first place for your sake, you know. But if I'd known you were going to be so ungrateful, I wouldn't have bothered." She turned to go.

"Gudrun, wait!"

Astrus took a step after her sister, but Gudrun turned with a snarl. "I want to be alone. I'm done with anything having to do with humans and their dogs." And with that, she stalked away.

An uncomfortable silence fell over them.

At last, Astrus shook her head and turned around. "Come on, I'll take you to the cave entrance at least."

The people started trekking back down the tunnel. Gless walked protectively close to Arthur's side, casting quick glances around, as if someone might try to take the Grail from them at any moment. Anwen walked between Bedivere and Lucan. And Cavall trailed behind with Astrus so that they could talk.

"I'm sorry about your sister," he said.

"Don't be." Astrus's tone was lighthearted, and slightly apologetic. "She just needs to calm down, that's all. Once she's less angry, we can talk again. We've put off talking about it for so long."

"Talking about what?" Cavall asked.

"The whole . . . guardians of the cave thing." Astrus sighed. "We've protected this cave for so long, but now I don't really see a reason to." She lifted her head, ears forward, as if she'd just had a thought. "When you leave . . ." She paused. "Would you consider taking me with you?"

He hadn't expected that. "Really? You want to come with us?"

"I don't want to be alone anymore. I want to leave the cave and see the world and meet more people. I want to see for myself, but . . ." She lowered her head, looking almost embarrassed. "I'd like to have someone to do it all with."

Cavall wagged his tail. He remembered the mix of fear

and excitement he'd felt when he'd first left his mother and littermates, the wide, unknown world waiting for him outside the farm. And the reassurance of knowing Arthur would be by his side through it all.

"Well, Lucan seems to like you," he said. "I know! If we can get Gelert's Wish to work, you can use it to ask him."

Astrus's mouth opened up into something almost like a smile. "Let me see if I can get it to work." She darted toward Arthur.

Gless tensed as she shot toward them but let her pass as she went for the hand with Gelert's Wish in it, not the Holy Grail. "Careful!" Cavall called after her. "People don't like teeth very much." Astrus seemed to have heard him, because instead of using her mouth, she nudged Arthur's hand with her nose.

Arthur looked down in surprise. "You want this?" He loosened his grip on the stone, and Astrus took it from him. He scratched his head with a look of growing confusion on his face as she then bounded over to Lucan. "I've never seen animals so excited over something they couldn't eat."

"What was that?" Lucan asked over his shoulder, just in

time to see Astrus hurtling toward him. Perhaps expecting her to knock him over, he threw up his hands to protect himself. Astrus skidded to a stop and dropped the stone at his feet.

"Lucan," she said, "I know you haven't known me long, and I know that our kind have not always gotten along so well, but I was hoping I could tell you—"

"What's this?" Lucan dropped his hands and bent down to pick up the stone.

The minute it was in his hand, the two of them froze. Astrus's fur stood on end, and her tail stuck straight out, rigid as a board. Lucan's eyes became wide. After a second, he turned to look at Astrus. Their eyes met.

"What's wrong?" Bedivere asked.

"Just now . . ." Lucan put a hand to his head. "I thought I felt a pull and . . ." He trailed off, looking frustrated. "Oh, it's nonsense."

"No." Bedivere gripped his brother's shoulder. "What is it?"

"I just *felt* as if this wolf wanted to thank me."

"You *felt* it?"

"I don't know. In my head? In my heart?" He shook his head. "I don't know," he repeated. "It was just a feeling. She wants to come with us."

Cavall came up to Astrus and nudged her. She jumped in surprise.

"What happened?" he asked.

"The same thing," she answered. "When he picked up the stone after I dropped it, I could *feel* that he wanted to thank me, too. I felt it like . . . like when lightning hits a tree."

"Ah." They both turned to see Gless, who was watching them with hooded eyes. He came forward. "I understand now."

"Understand what?" Cavall asked.

"The power of Gelert's Wish. It's not the power to *speak* with each other. It's the power to *understand* what the other wants to convey . . . what they're feeling."

"But . . . ," Cavall protested, thinking of all the times that Arthur had trusted him based on a shared look or how Arthur seemed to know when he needed comforting and vice versa when even the other people didn't seem to notice. "I can already do that with Arthur, and he can already do that with me."

"Then that's why it wouldn't work with you," Astrus said. "You two already understand each other without speaking."

Cavall stared at the ground, feeling his heart sink all the way to his feet. All of this, the reason he'd wanted to find the cave so badly in the first place, was for nothing.

No. He stopped himself before self-pity could set in. *That's not a good way to look at it. I came on this quest to help Arthur, and I have.* Arthur, who was patting his thigh to urge Cavall to keep up as they continued down the tunnel. And watching the way Astrus walked along with them, a happy skip in her step, made him realize how happy she was to have a special connection to a human— something he'd taken for granted before.

CHAPTER 20

AS THEY CONTINUED DOWN THE GLOWING TUN-
nel, Lucan walked with a renewed energy in
his step and a tuneless whistle on his lips.
Bedivere covered his ears with his hands. "What is that
terrible noise you're making?"

"It's the song of our quest. 'How the Brave Knights of
the Round Table Found the Holy Grail with the Help of
Astrus, the Brave Wolf.'"

"Perhaps you should leave the songwriting to the bards,"
Bedivere said.

"As well as the song name," Arthur added.

"And don't tell me," Bedivere continued, "that you've decided to *name* that animal."

"Of course," Lucan answered.

"But why Astrus?"

Lucan cocked his head. "I don't know," he replied with a shrug. "It just came to me, and it seems like a good name for a mysterious wolf."

Astrus trotted by his side, tail waving in the air. "I can't wait to tell Gudrun the good news," she said. "We're leaving this old cave behind."

"You think she'll want to come, too?" Cavall asked in surprise.

Astrus's eyes widened, as if she hadn't considered that before. "Oh, well . . . she probably won't," she admitted. "She'll probably want to stay here." Her tail drooped. "I suppose . . . I suppose I will have to stay here with her."

"You don't have to," Cavall said.

"I don't *have* to," Astrus agreed. "But Gudrun is my family, and I could never leave her all alone." She looked up at Lucan, who smiled back at her. "I hope Lucan understands."

Lucan had gone back to whistling, and Bedivere had

gone back to begging him to stop, but Cavall knew them both well enough now to recognize their good-natured, brotherly teasing.

"I'm sure he will," Cavall said.

Bedivere made a show of clamping his hands over his ears. "Arthur, are you sure the Grail hasn't been rattling my brother's mind?"

They laughed, and Lucan turned to face them with a scowl before finally laughing with them. "All right," he said, "I suppose I won't be becoming a bard myself any time soon, but . . ."

Arthur lifted a hand to silence him. "Shh."

Cavall heard it, too, up ahead. The horses were restless, scraping their hooves against the ground and snorting in agitation. As the group drew nearer, they found the three horses huddled together away from the cave entrance. Their eyes were wide.

"What's the matter with you?" Anwen snapped. "What's all this ruckus about?"

The horses looked at one another.

"The monster is still out there," Bedivere's horse said.

"It attacked me when I tried to graze," Arthur's horse said.

"Were you hurt?" Cavall asked.

Gless squinted at him like that was the stupidest question he'd ever asked.

"No," Arthur's horse said. "I got back to the cave before it could catch me. It wouldn't follow me inside, but it's been waiting out there ever since."

Cavall peered out from between the hanging vines at the cave's mouth. The forest lay beyond, the tall trees and fields of blue flowers, though he couldn't make out their color in the early morning darkness. "Where's the fog?"

Astrus seemed confused by his question, but then her ears perked up. "Oh, the obscuring magic. You broke its spell when you passed the Wolf Father's tests."

On the one paw, that meant they weren't in danger of getting lost in the mist, the way those men in the strange armor had been. On the other paw, it meant they couldn't rely on the mist to help them escape the garmr.

Gless growled low in his throat and crouched, legs coiled tightly and ready to spring. "We don't have time for this. I suggest we take care of this thing here and now."

"Me, too," Astrus said.

"How do we defeat it?" Cavall asked. "Arthur nearly took its head off with a sword, and that didn't seem to hurt it at all."

"Plus, the thing doesn't bleed," Anwen said. "It just . . . melts back together." She scrunched up her brow and looked to Gless. "Your person is the one who summoned it. Any suggestions on how to get rid of it?"

Gless sighed and closed his eyes. "It's a creature made of shadow. That's why it's strongest at dawn and dusk. Too much darkness and it can't take proper form, but too much light and it dissolves."

"That's why it won't come into the cave," Astrus agreed. "Do you think the light hurts it?"

"That might be it," Anwen said. "Remember the Night Mare, Cavall? It was made out of fire, and we defeated it with water. So maybe we can defeat this creature by drawing it into the light."

Astrus leveled her gaze upward at the patches of night sky visible through the vines. "It will be morning soon. Maybe we can distract it long enough for the sun to rise, catch it unaware."

"At the very least," Cavall said, "we can make sure it chases us while the horses get the people to safety."

Anwen raised her droopy eyes to the horses, who calmed down as the people soothed them. "Do you think you can manage that?" she asked skeptically. Of all the dogs, Anwen trusted horses the least, probably because she was most in danger of being run over by their hooves.

Arthur's horse snorted through his large nostrils. "Horses have greater stamina than dogs, as a rule," he said, using Anwen's same disdainful tone. "You create the distraction, and we'll take care of the rest."

Of course Arthur couldn't understand anything they were saying. He patted the horse along the muzzle. "The horses should be fresh to ride," he said to the others. "I'll take the Grail and go on ahead. You two can rest here with the dogs, if you'd like."

"With all due honor, Your Highness," Bedivere said, "I would *not* like."

"We'll ride with you," Lucan added. "If, of course, we won't slow you down."

"And even if we were to slow you down," Bedivere

continued, "we'd insist on accompanying you in any case. That great beast is still out there, after all."

Arthur nodded. "I thought you might say as much. Very well, then. We head out immediately." He strapped the bag with the Holy Grail and Gelert's Wish onto his horse's pack, then checked the reins and saddle before mounting up. "You've earned a long rest, too, my friend," he said, patting the horse's neck. "When we get back to Camelot, I'll have the stable hands brush you down and give you all the fresh apples you can eat. How does that sound?"

"Heavenly," the horse replied.

As the people got the horses ready, Astrus and the dogs crept to the opening of the cave and peered out. "We'll run out together," Anwen said, "and let it chase us a while. Then we'll split up. That'll confuse it even more. By the time it chooses one of us to chase, the people will have escaped." Her eyebrows scrunched up. "Hopefully."

"What if they don't leave us?" Astrus asked.

Cavall worried about that, too. "The horses know our plan and will make sure they escape. Besides, people are pretty smart. They'll probably be able to see what we're trying to do. We'll just have to trust that they trust us."

"I will go with them," Gless said. "I have a vested interest in seeing the Grail gets back to Camelot. I will protect the people carrying it, should your plan fail."

Cavall looked at Gless, and his brother met his gaze. There was no challenge in Gless's eyes now, though, just a grim determination. "I trust you," Cavall said.

Gless nodded in what might have been gratitude or simple acknowledgment; it was difficult to tell with him.

Over the trees, the black of the night sky slowly gave way to dark blue, signaling the sun's imminent rise. Long shadows began to stretch between the trees. The forest was unnaturally still for being so close to daytime. No birds chirped, and no leaves rustled. It was eerie. Cavall steeled himself.

"On my mark," Anwen said, crouching low. She looked out through the ferns obscuring the cave entrance and lifted her nose one last time. "Go!" she cried.

CHAPTER 21

HE PEOPLE SHOUTED IN ALARM AS THE DOGS
burst into a run. The moment they were
out of the crystals' glowing protection, the
shadows just beyond the cave began to twist and writhe.
A shape took form, larger than it had been before, bulk-
ier, with two enormous horns jutting from its head. The
garmr had returned in the form of a massive bull.

It charged at them faster than Cavall had anticipated,
thundering on hooves that seemed to shake the very forest.
Cavall put as much strength as he could into his legs. His
friends depended on him not to fall behind. The creature

roared as it veered toward them. Its breath blew hot against their heels as their paths converged.

A loud yelp rang out off to Cavall's left, and he turned his head in time to see Astrus crash to the ground. Cavall's legs carried him several more paces before he could grind to a halt. He spun. There was a triumphant glint in the shadow creature's eyes as it lowered its horns and aimed for the fallen wolf.

Cavall dug his paws in, ready to go back to Astrus's aid, but someone else beat him to it. Gudrun burst from the cave entrance, fur flashing in the slashes of light through the trees. She sank her teeth into the garmr's whiplike tail and pulled. It bellowed and turned on her, away from Astrus.

"That's right," Gudrun said mockingly. "After me. This way." She took off running in the opposite direction. The garmr followed.

Astrus climbed to her feet as Cavall and Anwen reached her. "We have to go after her," Astrus said, staggering a few steps before she regained her pace. "Gudrun may act tough, but she'll never be able to take on that thing by herself." Without waiting for an answer, she took off after her sister.

Cavall agreed. He went off after Astrus, and Anwen after him.

Something came rushing up behind them, leaving a strong wind in its wake. It was Bedivere on his horse, sword held aloft. He wove his way between the trees, following on the trail of Gudrun and the garmr. Cavall gaped. The people were supposed to have run the *other* direction. If Bedivere got there before them, they would need to rescue him *and* Gudrun now.

Cavall, Anwen, and Astrus gave chase, but Arthur's horse had been right: horses had greater stamina. Bedivere was faster than them, disappearing into the copse of trees along with the garmr and Gudrun.

A moment later, a howl of pain erupted from the bushes ahead.

"Gudrun!" Astrus cried.

They burst through the undergrowth in time to see Bedivere charge the garmr. The weapon cut deeply into the bull's shoulder. The monster screamed and folded in on itself. It began to change again. Its horns turned to fangs; its four legs became eight. It had become the largest spider Cavall had ever seen, easily as big as a wolf. It hissed and lunged at Bedivere, who waved his sword about to draw its attention away from its intended target: Gudrun. She lay on her side, unmoving, a gaping wound on her back.

Astrus ran to her side while Anwen ran to help Bedivere. Cavall threw himself into the fray, latching onto one of its spindly legs with his teeth. The creature shrieked and shook him free with ease. He backed off, not wanting another bite to his paw. Or any part of him, really.

The monster chased after him, but in doing so made the mistake of turning its back on Anwen. It was taken completely by surprise as she barreled headlong into it from behind. She struck hard. The spider toppled over like a giant, hairy boulder. Eight legs kicked in the air as it screamed and struggled to right itself.

"Keep it busy," Cavall panted. "We have to give Bedivere enough time to . . ." He trailed off as he looked over his shoulder. Bedivere had not ridden off. He'd brought his horse around, dismounted, and was now leaning over

Gudrun, his hand pressed to the wound on her back. No, he shouldn't be here. He should be back on his horse, riding as far away from here as fast as he could.

Unfortunately, Cavall shouldn't have let his guard down either by turning his back. "Cavall!" Anwen shouted in warning, giving Cavall just enough time to dodge the garmr's next attack. Spider fangs lashed out. If his tail had been just a few inches longer, he'd have suffered a nasty bite. Good thing he'd already lost those extra inches to the Night Mare.

As he regained his senses, Arthur and Lucan, astride their horses, burst through the trees. Gless ran between them.

"Gless!"

His brother hardly slowed at all, joining in the charge at the garmr.

"Gless," Cavall tried again, "you need to get the people out of here. It's not safe."

"Trust me, Cavall," Gless growled, eyes locked on the beast. "I promise, as long as your person is the only way to get the Grail back to Camelot, I will protect him. And we've already established I'm the most honest one among us."

Cavall thought he saw his brother wink at him, but he couldn't be sure, because at that moment the people charged the beast.

Arthur held aloft Excalibur, even though he had to have known it would do no good. He delivered a kick to the garmr that sent it staggering back a mere pace or two, only to huddle in on itself and re-form, once again into a wolf. "Our weapons won't harm it," Arthur called to Lucan, who looked ready to strike with his own sword.

"Then how *do* we harm it?" Lucan said through gritted teeth.

"I don't know." Arthur pulled his horse out of the way as the shadow beast ran in for another attack.

Gless headed it off, snapping with a fury that surprised even Cavall. He couldn't just stand there doing nothing, though. He had to let the people know the garmr's weakness. Using Gless's distraction, he barked to get Arthur's attention. Arthur swung his head around, and his eyes locked with Cavall's. Good. Now what?

His mind raced. Gless continued to fight with the

monster, and Cavall didn't have much time to get Arthur to understand.

Cavall crouched down in the shadow of the tree, then quickly hopped back into the light.

Arthur bunched up his brows in confusion, but he was still paying attention, so that was good.

Cavall darted into the next shadow, paused, then ran back into the light. His heart pounded as he willed Arthur to understand.

Arthur's eyebrows shot up. "The light!"

Cavall's heart swelled to fill his chest. Yes, his person understood!

"The creature is weak in the light!" Arthur yelled over the stomping of hooves and gnashing of teeth; both Bedivere and Lucan turned their heads at his voice. "That's why it wouldn't follow us into the cave."

"Then we retreat," Lucan said. "Bedivere, back on your horse. We're returning to the cave."

"No, wait." Bedivere held up his hand. "Can you keep it distracted for a few moments?"

"Why?" Lucan asked.

"Just trust me."

"I trust you," Arthur called, swinging Excalibur furiously back and forth, just barely keeping the creature at bay. "But you'd best hurry. I don't know how long I can keep it 'distracted' like this."

"Just a little bit longer." Bedivere, still crouched by Gudrun's side, gave the wolf a reassuring smile. "You can hold on just a little bit longer, can't you, old girl?"

Gudrun didn't respond, and Cavall hoped it wasn't already too late.

Bedivere reached for a fallen tree branch, hardly more than a stick. Did he intend to use that as a weapon? If so, he should choose a larger one. Even stranger, he snapped it in two and began rubbing them together furiously. Cavall didn't have time to wonder about it, though. If Arthur trusted Bedivere's plan, then Cavall did, too, and would do everything he could to buy the knight more time.

Cavall and the other dogs rushed in again, but if the people's swords couldn't do any damage, there seemed little hope for them. Right now, the best he could do was shield his person from the monster's teeth. He threw himself between Arthur and the garmr, taking several bites to his side. The pain was worse than when his paw had been wounded, but he continued to fight.

He charged at the garmr, flinging himself at it with wild abandon. It became a ram, then a bear, then a wolf again. Claws swiped at his shoulder; teeth bit into his back. It didn't matter how much damage he took as long as they had the Holy Grail to heal him, as long as he could continue to fight to protect Arthur. He would continue to heal himself just as this creature continued to re-form itself. He would keep fighting forever if he needed to. There was no way he would let this monster harm any more of his friends.

"Gah!" The sudden noise startled Cavall. Bedivere came rushing in with a lit torch he had fashioned hastily from the tree branch. The smoke from the glowing flame was hot and thick, choking the air with the smell of burning wood. Cavall moved out of its way.

The creature stared in confusion as Bedivere ran straight for it, never slowing. As he ran, Bedivere hefted the torch over his head and let it fly. It tumbled end over end in an elegant arc and landed soundlessly on the beast's back.

The garmr howled as its fur caught on fire. Well, no, it didn't really catch on fire, not the way most things caught on fire. Rather, its fur seemed to dissolve under the flames, turning to smoke. The creature fell to the ground and began rolling in a desperate attempt to extinguish itself, to no avail. Wherever the flames spread, the creature's body vanished, like darkness from a room when the curtains were drawn.

The creature's glowing eyes rolled in its head as it realized its impending doom. It lifted its head as the flames drew nearer. A mournful wail rose from its throat before dying out.

And then it was gone.

Vanished, as if it had never been there.

 VERYONE STARED AT WHERE THE GARMR HAD vanished. Then Lucan stumbled from his horse and ran to smack Bedivere on the head.

"Ow! What was that for?"

"For running off to fight that beast by yourself," Lucan said.

Bedivere rubbed at his head, but he didn't look truly hurt. "I could not let that creature harm the beasts who saved my brother's life."

Arthur unslung his horse's pack and rummaged around inside until he found the Holy Grail. "Are the both of you all right? Do either of you need healing?" he asked. Bedivere and Lucan shook their heads, so Arthur turned to Cavall. "What a troublesome dog you are to need the powers of the Holy Grail twice in one day."

Cavall wagged his tail. He could tell by the smile on Arthur's face that he was just teasing. But he couldn't accept the offer, not while Gudrun was still badly hurt. She was still breathing, evidenced by the slow rise and fall of her chest, but she needed the Grail more than any of them. He limped over to her side and nudged her with his nose.

Arthur looked over his shoulder. "Ah," he said in understanding. "Of course."

"May I?" Bedivere asked, holding out his hands.

Arthur nodded and handed him the Grail.

Bedivere filled it from his own water skin and carried it with steady hands over to Gudrun. Cavall and Astrus, who had been standing over her sister, took a step back to allow Bedivere to kneel. Gudrun lifted her head; it looked like it cost her great effort to do so. Wordlessly, Bedivere brought the cup to her muzzle, and she drank.

The copse was quiet. Then the notes of a birdsong drifted down from the tree branches overhead, and the other sounds of the forest began to return as well.

Gudrun rolled over and pushed herself up onto shaky paws. Blood matted her back and flank, but no wound remained.

"Gudrun!" Astrus rushed in and licked her sister's face.

A deep sigh caused Cavall to look down to see Anwen releasing a breath of relief. She caught Cavall staring and frowned. "I wasn't worried, you know," she grumbled.

Bedivere carried the Grail back to Arthur. "Now you can heal Cavall . . . again." He began to chuckle, but stopped short. "What's that?" he asked, pointing to something on the ground. A stone with a dog's paw surrounded by etched symbols—Gelert's Wish.

"Ah, something Cavall took a liking to," Arthur answered. "Must have fallen out when I unpacked the Grail."

Bedivere bent down to pick it up. "Odd. It can't be worth much, especially to a dog."

"I wonder who will use it now," Astrus commented idly. Cavall gave her a questioning look. "I mean, now that you know you can't use it on Arthur." She sighed. "I hope some other dog gets to use it. It really is an incredible feeling, bonding with a person like that."

Gudrun grunted, and Cavall thought she would scold her sister for saying such a thing. Instead, she limped forward to Bedivere and leaned against him. Bedivere went completely stiff. He even stopped breathing when Gudrun reached up with her mouth and took the stone from his hands. The minute her muzzle touched Gelert's Wish, both she and Bedivere jolted, just as had happened with Astrus and Lucan. Gudrun, at least, looked like she had expected such a reaction and recovered quickly. She dropped the stone and began to lick Bedivere's hand.

"Bedivere," Arthur said, brows scrunched together, "are you all right?"

"I . . . am fine." Bedivere put one hand to his head as Gudrun continued to lick his other hand. "I had a strange feeling just now."

Arthur raised his eyebrows.

"Do you remember when I said I would know my dog when I met it?"

"Yes."

Bedivere looked down at Gudrun and slowly brought his free hand to stroke through the fur on her neck. "I feel like I've found her."

CHAPTER 23

HE JOURNEY BACK WAS A BLUR. THE FIELDS OF blue flowers, the mossy, twisted trees, the babbling brook—it all passed by in the blink of an eye. Arthur pushed his horse, and everyone else had to run to keep up with him. Luckily, nothing else bothered them during the day, and they rested at night so as not to run afoul of any unfriendly fay. Arthur refused to go to sleep until Cavall sat on his chest to get him to lie down. Then he'd be asleep in a matter of minutes, he was that tired. Astrus and Gudrun took up watch duties with the dogs, which allowed all of the humans more time to rest.

Gless hung around the perimeter of the camp, as he had on the journey out, silent but tense with nervous energy that set even Cavall on edge.

"Not going to talk to any puddles?" Anwen teased him.

He regarded her darkly for a moment, then sighed. "I suppose I owe you an explanation about that." He snorted, as if having to explain himself was a chore he'd rather not do. "I was trying to contact Mordred."

"Through puddles?" Cavall asked.

"Through anything that casts a reflection," Gless replied. "Surfaces that reflect have the ability to allow magic users to speak with each other across vast distances."

A quick memory came to Cavall—Mordred peering into a bucket of water, Morgana's voice answering him back.

Gless shook his head. "But he wouldn't answer me. Even with my power as his familiar, I couldn't find him." He hunched over, looking about as miserable as Cavall had ever seen him. "The idiot. I *told* him not to play with magic. None of this would have happened if he had just *listened* to me."

It struck Cavall then. Gless and Mordred could speak to each other, but what good was that when they wouldn't listen to each other?

On the third day, they reached the road again, which made traveling faster and easier. The people rode out ahead, but for the first time, Gudrun held back. Astrus stopped and turned back for her sister. "What's wrong?" she asked. "Are you having second thoughts?"

"I've been *having* second thoughts," Gudrun muttered. "And third thoughts. And fourth thoughts. But seeing the human road made me realize . . . things are going to be different from now on, aren't they?"

"Yes," Astrus said. "We don't have to go through with this, though. If you don't want to live with the people . . ." She trailed off.

"She's right. You always have a choice," Cavall said, even though he hoped Gudrun wouldn't change her mind. He'd been looking forward to the wolf sisters coming to live with them at the castle.

Gudrun shook her head. "No, I've already decided. It's just . . ." Her expression changed into one Cavall hadn't seen on her before. She looked nervous. "I'm scared," she admitted.

Astrus nuzzled her. "It's all right to be scared," she said. "I'm a little scared myself. But everything will be all right as long as we're together."

Gudrun nuzzled her back, and Cavall felt suddenly jealous. He wished he had that sort of relationship with his own brother. He wished Arthur had that sort of relationship with Mordred. Why was family always more complicated than friendship?

The forest fell behind them, and ahead of them lay the road. And at the end of the road stood the castle, looking as large as the first time Cavall had laid eyes on it. They stood there, dirty and dusty and worn ragged, with the tall spires beckoning them home. Home. That was a nice feeling.

As they drew nearer, Cavall saw two birds flying high overhead—a falcon and a snowy owl. Cavall had never seen an owl out in daylight before, and the falcon appeared to be carrying a staff in its talons. But just as he wondered on it, the two birds changed angle and flew straight for them.

The falcon swooped down and alit on the road right in

front of them. Its wings turned to flowing robes; its beak became a crooked nose. In an instant, the bird had become Merlin, leaning heavily on his walking staff.

"I think I have had quite enough of shape-shifters for a while," Bedivere muttered as the people began to dismount their horses to meet the wizard.

Merlin chuckled as he drew near. "My friend here saw you on the road and told me you would be arriving shortly." Cavall followed his gaze to the snowy owl, who flew past them, powerful wings beating as it headed for the trees. "Though I'm afraid Archimedes is not very social." Merlin shook his head. "He also told me you had two new friends with you." He bowed his head to the wolves. "It is a pleasure to meet you, Gudrun and Astrus."

The sisters looked at him in surprise.

"I knew your Wolf Father, a long time ago. I also know that he would approve highly of you leaving behind a path you did not care for and instead making your own."

"You . . . knew our ancestor?" Gudrun asked.

Merlin nodded. "Loki and I were . . . *are* family." The corners of his eyes crinkled. "So I suppose, in a way, that makes *us* family as well."

This time the sisters looked at each other.

"And I believe," Merlin continued, motioning toward the castle in the distance, "that you will find even more family in Camelot."

"Merlin!" Arthur hopped down from his horse and ran to Merlin's side. "Mordred, is he—?"

Merlin raised his hand. "He still lives. Gwen is tending him as we speak, but he holds on by a single thread."

Arthur gripped the old man by the shoulders. "I found it, Merlin. I found the Holy Grail."

Merlin placed a hand on top of Arthur's. "Then let us not delay any longer."

The sun had just set by the time they got to the castle, and despite the time, everyone had gathered in the courtyard to welcome them home. Banners blew in an easy breeze. A horn blared a jubilant note. People shouted and cheered and crowded in around the returning party.

"I've never seen so many people before," Astrus said, hanging back with Gudrun.

Lucan noticed this and nudged his brother. "Arthur," he called, "go see to your son. Bedivere and I will take care of things out here." He pushed his way out of the crowd and knelt down, hand held out to the wolves. "And we will take care of you as well, my friends."

Astrus took a step forward and licked his hand. He reached out and petted her head.

Cavall watched this scene from across the courtyard, before Arthur's frantic searching through his horse's packs for the Grail brought his attention back to the matter at hand. "Will you be all right?" he called to the wolves.

Gudrun's eyes met his. "We will be fine," she answered, nodding to Arthur. "Go, be with your person."

Cavall nodded in gratitude and followed Arthur as he hurried into the castle. Gless was already ahead of him, pausing every few steps to look over his shoulder, urging Arthur to hurry up.

When they reached the room, the smell of sweat and sickness assaulted Cavall's nose. Mordred was right where they'd left him on his bed, but now he was very thin, very pale, and covered in a layer of sweat. Gless ran to his side and sat, staring intently at his person.

Gwen sat on the bed, looking as if she'd been getting

ready for bed—her hair was down and she wore a night-gown under her robe. Luwella lay at her feet. They both rose when Arthur entered, and Gwen ran to him and wrapped her arms around his neck to pull him in for a hug. He hugged her back and they touched lips. "I worried about you," she said. "But I knew you would come back to me."

Arthur opened his mouth, and Cavall could guess what he wanted to ask. Gwen must have known, too, because she answered before he could say a word.

"Mordred is still alive, but he is not well. The physician has been giving him water and broth when he can, but he grows weaker every day." She finally let go of him and took a step back. "He spoke in his sleep. He called out for you."

"Is it true?" Cavall asked Luwella. "Did Mordred really call out for Arthur?" That didn't seem like something Gwen would lie about.

"He was callink out for his mother more often," Luwella replied. "But yes, he did say 'Father' several times."

Arthur made his way to the bed and brushed the wet hair from Mordred's forehead. "Could someone bring water?" His voice trembled.

As the physician went to fetch water, Cavall came up and leaned against Arthur's legs. Arthur took a deep breath, and the shaking of his limbs went away. He took the Holy Grail from his pack just as the physician returned with a bowl of water.

Arthur dipped the Grail in and filled it to the sloshing point. His hands shook so badly, Gwen took the cup from him. Arthur gave her a thankful nod and gathered Mordred in his arms. Mordred looked small and defenseless like that, Cavall thought as he watched, and not at all like a threat to Arthur and Camelot. When Mordred was in a sitting position, Gwen came forward, holding the Grail. She looked hesitant at first, but then put the Grail to Mordred's lips and tilted the water in. More of it ran down his chin and onto his nightshirt than actually went into his mouth. Some made it, though, from the way Mordred's throat bobbed.

When the cup was empty, Gwen stepped back and everyone watched.

One moment passed. Then another.

Slowly, Mordred's eyes began fluttering.

Gless's ears perked up.

"Quickly, more," Arthur said.

Gwen filled the cup again and repeated the motion. This time, more water went down Mordred's throat. He made a loud groaning noise, and then he opened his eyes. They were unfocused at first, but then landed on Gwen holding the Grail. "Gw . . . en?" He craned his neck and looked up at Arthur. "Father?"

Gless hopped onto the bed, tail wagging. He made to lick Mordred's face, then stopped, as if realizing others were watching him. He quickly calmed himself and sat on Mordred's legs, trying to look aloof and uninterested.

"Gless?" Mordred reached out a shaky hand and awkwardly patted Gless's back, as if making sure he was really there.

Arthur pulled Mordred into a tight hug. "Welcome back."

Cavall could see Mordred's confused face over Arthur's shoulder. "But . . . how . . . ?" His voice sounded as weak and thin as his body.

Gwen smiled at him. "Your father loves you very much. Someday I hope you realize just *how* much."

CHAPTER 24

HERE WAS A FEAST THAT NIGHT. ARTHUR SAID it was in honor of Mordred's recovery, Gwen said it was in honor of Arthur and the knights' safe return, and the knights said it was in honor of a quest nobly fulfilled. If it were up to Cavall, though, it would be in honor of their new friends. Only, Astrus and Gudrun had been sent to the stables for the time being. Apparently not everyone was eager to welcome the wolves inside just yet.

Through all the laughing and clinking of cups and food being passed around, Cavall couldn't stop thinking about them out there. They should be in here, enjoying the merriment, even if the other dogs thought they were crazy for bringing wolves back to Camelot. Anwen tried to convince them that the quest surely would have failed without the sisters' help, but they remained skeptical. Luwella would need the most convincing, but she was a wolfhound, after all; in her homeland, she had hunted wolves especially. Edelm listened to their recounting of events with a thoughtful look on his face but said nothing. In his prime, Edelm had probably hunted plenty of wolves himself, so it would take time for him to get used to the idea of living with them. Cavall was glad that Anwen was standing up for them. He was also glad that she did most of the talking. He didn't feel much like socializing.

Gless didn't either, judging by the way he had rooted himself to Mordred's feet at his chair. Mordred's hands shook as he ate—and ate and ate and ate—and plenty of food fell from the table, but Gless never made any move to snatch it up. Not even the juicy bits of ham from the large pig that served as the centerpiece of the feast. His brother had a stern look on his face, but Cavall couldn't forget the way his tail had started wagging when Mordred had come awake.

"Glad to see you back among the living, lad." Bedivere slapped Mordred's back jovially. "Do you mind if I just . . ." He reached over him and began loading up his plate with ham. "Never mind me."

"Careful, Bedivere," Gwen chided with a thin smile on her lips. "You'll turn into a pig yourself eating like that. Mordred, at least, has an excuse."

"Oh, let him have as much as he wants," Arthur said. "Returning knights may make pigs of themselves if they wish, and my knights have certainly earned it." He leaned over and touched his lips against her cheek. Gwen rolled her eyes, but she smiled and looked happier than she had since she'd first heard of Mordred's accident. Perhaps she, like Cavall, was happy that Arthur was happy again, even if it meant Mordred would return to being a thoroughly nasty person.

"Actually, Your Majesties," Bedivere said, standing, "I hope you won't mind me excusing myself, but I can think of two others who deserve it as much as me."

"Of course," Arthur said with a nod.

Cavall followed after Bedivere as he made his way through hallways of servants coming and going with trays of food and pitchers of wine. They left the noise of the feast behind them and made their way to the kitchens, where the door opened to the outside to let the night air cool off the overheated ovens. From there, it was a quick walk across the courtyard to the kennels.

Astrus and Gudrun ran up to the gate to meet him. "Sorry, girls," Bedivere said. "You're stuck out here while we're all celebrating inside. But I brought something to make it up to you. A little." He crouched down and held out the plate of steaming ham for them to see.

"What is it?" Gudrun asked. She sounded uncertain, but saliva dripped from her mouth all the same.

"Whatever it is, it smells wonderful." Astrus took the first bite. "It is. It is wonderful. Have some."

"But what *is* it?"

"It's ham," Cavall answered.

Gudrun looked at him through the bars of the kennel gate. "And what sort of animal is a ham?"

"It's . . . well, it's not an animal, exactly. It's a type of meat from a pig."

"Oh, well, why didn't you say so in the first place?" Gudrun joined Astrus in devouring the rest of the plate. They were done with it in the blink of an eye, and afterward, Gudrun licked her chops to get the last bits off. "That *was* wonderful," she said. "Not like any pig I've ever had."

"It's been cooked."

"Is that how all food is here?" Astrus asked.

"Most of the time," Cavall answered. "I once ate an uncooked chicken from the kitchen and the people yelled at me. I think eating uncooked meat isn't looked upon very highly among people."

"It will take some getting used to," Gudrun said, "but I like it. I like it a lot." She looked up at Bedivere through the slats of the kennel.

"There's a bit more on my fingers. I'll let you lick it off." Bedivere began to hold his hand out, then stopped. "If you promise not to bite my fingers off."

"I promise," she said.

Bedivere looked startled for a moment. He blinked, then shook his head. "Guess I need a good night's rest better than I thought," he muttered to himself. "I'm hearing things." He held his hand out toward the slats, close enough that Gudrun could reach with her tongue but far enough that she couldn't reach with her teeth.

He didn't have any reason to worry, though, because Gudrun was gentle as she licked the remaining ham bits from his fingers.

When she was done, Bedivere stood. "Aye, you're a good girl. We'll see about moving you into the castle soon enough. But for now, I'll be by to see you in the morning. No doubt my brother will, too." He gave a yawn, blinked, and shook his head again. "Good night." With one last wave to the wolves, he turned and headed back for the glow from the kitchen door.

Cavall took his spot in front of the pen. "Are you comfortable in there?"

"Comfortable enough," Gudrun answered. "Beats sleeping in a cave."

"We're very comfortable," Astrus said.

"Good. Because if you ever change your mind, all you need to do is tell me and—"

"Thank you," Astrus interrupted. "But I can't very well go back now that I've had a taste of ham, can I?"

"I suppose not," Cavall agreed.

They bid each other good night, and Cavall turned to go. He was hungry himself from the smells wafting from the kitchens. Now that he wasn't so worried about Gudrun and Astrus, he could take his place below Arthur's chair and gobble up the food that hit the floor. His tail wagged at the prospect.

"I see you have returned safely from your journey."

At the threshold of the kitchen door, Cavall froze at the unexpected voice, but relaxed when he smelled Drudwyn. He turned to see the odd dog emerge from the shadows near the stables at a light trot.

"Do you have a moment? I don't wish to keep you from your celebration feast."

"Oh, it's not my feast," Cavall protested.

"Nonsense. It's your feast as much as anyone else's. Perhaps more."

Cavall glanced toward the kitchen, where the smell of food beckoned him. Well, there was a lot of food at the table; they probably wouldn't run out too quickly. He supposed he could stay and talk with Drudwyn for a bit.

They settled down outside the kitchen, light spilling out through the open doorway.

"Drudwyn, I found it," Cavall said. "I found Gelert's Wish. It was just like you said. Well, not *just* like you said. It doesn't give people and dogs the ability to *speak* with each other, but—"

"Slow down," Drudwyn said with a chuckle.

"It's kind of funny, really," Cavall continued, forcing himself to slow down. He couldn't help it. His mind raced faster than his words could keep up with. "You told me the story of Gelert's Wish right before we went on a quest that ended up taking us right to it. Isn't that an odd coincidence?"

"An odd coincidence indeed," Drudwyn agreed.

Cavall paused. A new thought occurred to him, but it was strange, and he didn't want Drudwyn to laugh at him for being stupid. "Did you . . . know we were going to find

Gelert's Wish when you told me that story?" No, that was a silly question.

"How could I have possibly known that?" Drudwyn said. "But this world of ours is strange and infinitely mysterious. Perhaps you were meant to find Gelert's Wish. Perhaps you would not have found it if I hadn't told you that exact story at that exact time."

Now Cavall felt confused.

"I'm sorry," Drudwyn said, "I don't mean to speak in riddles. I didn't call you away from your well-deserved celebration to confuse you."

"Then what do you want to talk to me about?" Cavall asked. "Did you want to tell me one of your stories?"

"No." Drudwyn lowered his body to the ground, making himself comfortable. "I'd rather *you* tell *me* a story, Cavall."

"Me? But I don't know any stories."

"Of course you do." Drudwyn gave him a sly, sideways look. "You just lived one. A great story, by the sounds of it."

"You want to hear about what happened on the quest?"

"I told you, I am a rememberer of stories, and I am

always looking for new stories to remember." His tail thumped against the floor. It was perhaps the first genuinely doglike thing Cavall had ever seen him do. "Won't you give me another story to remember?"

Acknowledgments

I had just as many people helping me on Cavall's second adventure as on his first.

First, I'd like to thank my agents, Lauren Galit Knight and Caitlen Rubino-Bradway at LKG Agency, for always helping me develop thoughts into ideas, and my editor at HarperCollins, Rose Pleuler, for helping me develop ideas into plot.

Secondly, I want to thank all the friends who helped me along the way. Andrea Hurst, an incredible friend, mentor, and fellow dog lover. Mike McNeff, Derrick Sutton, and all the members of my writing group, as well as Dave and Pat for hosting us every Monday at the Salty Mug on the wharf.

And lastly, thank you to my family—all the aunts, uncles, and cousins from both the Mackamans and Lautenbachs. I would love to thank you all by name, but we all know that would take a whole book unto itself. So suffice to say, thank you to everyone who's supported me, whether we're related through blood or good times. And to my parents, Dave and Laura Mackaman, and my brother, Will Mackaman, who all taught me love is so much more than what you say; it's how you show it.

Books by

AUDREY MACKAMAN

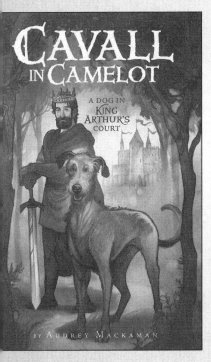

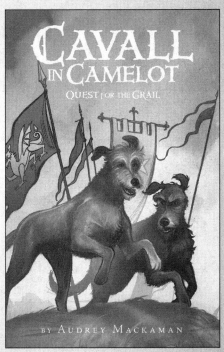

HARPER
Imprint of HarperCollinsPublishers

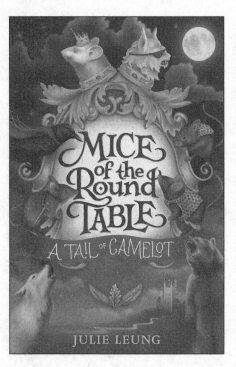
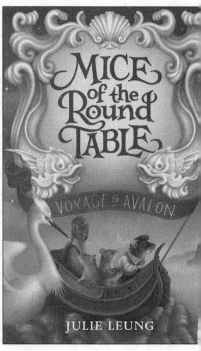